dOg days

the misadventures of Willie Plummet

PAUL BUCHANAN
& ROD RANDALL

CPH
SAINT LOUIS

The Misadventures of Willie Plummet

Cover illustration by John Ward.
Back cover photo by Ira Lippke.
Cover and interior design by Karol Bergdolt.

Copyright © 1999 Paul Buchanan
Published by Concordia Publishing House
3558 S. Jefferson Avenue, St. Louis, MO 63118-3968
Manufactured in the United States of America

Library of Congress Cataloging-in-Publication Data

2   3   4   5   6   7   8   9   10   08   07   06   05   04   03   02   01   00

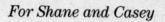

For Shane and Casey

Contents

I suppose I was getting on Mom's nerves being underfoot all day. At about three in the afternoon she came in the living room and switched off "The Animaniacs." I'd been lying on the sofa with my head hanging over the edge, watching cartoons upside down; it made them a bit more interesting. I looked up at Mom from where I lay with my feet hanging over the back of the sofa and my head dangling near the floor.

"I need you to do something, Willie," she told me. She seemed kind of mad, but I thought maybe that was just how she looked upside down.

I sat up. She still looked mad.

"I need you to go down the street to Mrs. Lawton's house and see how she's doing."

I scratched my head. It was itchy from hanging upside down. "See how she's doing?"

"That's what I said," Mom told me. "Go see how she's doing."

"Can I wait till later, when it starts cooling down?" I asked. "It's really hot outside." It was the dog days of August, and Glenfield had been going through a major heat wave. Records had been broken nearly every day that week. I'd spent all those days lying around the air-conditioned house, drinking Mom's iced tea and watching television. The last thing I wanted to do right now was go outside.

"That's the whole point," Mom said. "Old people can get very sick when the temperature gets too high. If we don't check on Mrs. Lawton, who will?"

I was about to suggest to Mom that she just call Mrs. Lawton on the phone to see if she was okay, but I could tell from Mom's expression that my convenience wasn't really the issue here. She wanted the house to be Willie-free for a few minutes.

I guess Mom was right. If *we* didn't check on Mrs. Lawton, who would? No one seemed to go near the old lady's house. Sometimes I'd see her out walking in the mornings. She'd be on her way to the park on Pickett Avenue when I was on my way to school, and I'd wave to her. Sometimes I'd see her coming out of the early service at church when we were going in for the late one, and we'd all say hello. Otherwise she spent most of her time alone inside her big house.

Mom went over to Mrs. Lawton's house every week or two for a visit, but no one else in the neighborhood did. Even Mrs. Lawton's son hardly visited. I only saw his white Mercedes in her driveway a few times each year, even though he lived just over in Cedarville.

"Okay," I said. "But when I knock on the door and she opens it, what do I say? I'll feel like a dork."

"Just ask her if there's anything she needs," Mom told me. "She'll appreciate the thought."

The heat hit me as soon as I opened the front door and stepped out onto the porch. It was suddenly hard to breathe. I walked across the lawn, and the grass was dry and brittle. By the time I reached the sidewalk, I was already sweating. I headed up the street toward Mrs. Lawton's house. I could feel the heat of the sidewalk through the soles of my tennis shoes. Half way down the block, I felt the warmth of the sun pressing down on my shoulders like a weight, like the sun was burning straight through my T-shirt. No one was on the streets, and all the curtains in the windows were drawn.

Mrs. Lawton's house was down on the corner. It was much bigger and older than any of the other houses in the neighborhood, and you could tell by the way our street curved it had been bent to pass around her property. Mom said the house had been in the Lawton family for generations.

The broad front steps were wooden and worn, and they groaned as I climbed them. I hoped it would be a bit cooler in the shade of the house's huge front porch, but it wasn't. I passed an old porch swing and stepped up to the huge front door. Big brass house numbers were attached along the top of the door frame with tiny screws: 26343. I wiped my damp hand on my shorts and gave the big brass knocker a couple of sharp knocks.

A small dog started scraping and yapping on the other side of the heavy door, but no other sounds came from inside. At first I felt relieved that Mrs. Lawton wasn't home; I could go back to my air conditioning and "The Animaniacs." Then it struck me that maybe Mrs. Lawton was hard of hearing. Maybe she hadn't *heard* me knock. I gave the knocker another couple of sharp raps. There was more barking, but still no answer.

At that point I started to worry. I remembered Mom said old people can have health problems when the temperature gets too high. I'd seen it on the news all the time, and, of course, that's why Mom sent me here in the first place. What if Mrs. Lawton *couldn't* answer the door? I pictured her lying on a sofa too weak to move. It was a scary thought, but it was possible.

At first I thought I'd run home and get Mom, but she was already ticked at me. It would be a week before I saw another cartoon if I dragged her outside on a day like this, in a panic, to find Mrs. Lawton sipping iced tea on the back porch. I wasn't sure what to do.

I pressed my ear to the heavy front door. All I could hear on the other side was a scratching way down low. I knocked again as loudly as I could. The dog yelped and barked. I waited a few seconds and then tried the door knob. The door was locked, and to tell the truth, I was relieved—I wouldn't have to decide whether to enter uninvited.

I went to the two big windows that looked out on the porch and cupped my hands against the glass. I tried to peek through, terrified that I'd see Mrs. Lawton passed out on the floor. Behind the lace curtains, the blinds were drawn tight. I couldn't see a thing. I went back to the front door and banged on it with the side of my fist as hard as I could. I guess I banged a little too hard. The brass 2 fell off the door frame and clanked on the wooden porch floor, just missing my foot. I glanced up at her house number. It was now 6343.

When I bent down to pick up the brass 2, I noticed there was a crack between the porch floor and the bottom of the door. I could hear the dog sniffing down there. Maybe the crack was big enough for me to see inside. I got down on my knees and peeked under the door. I could see tiny dog claws frantically scrambling around, but not much more. I lay flat on my stomach for a better look. I pressed my eye to the crack. Besides the dog's paws, I saw two dark shapes that seemed to be moving. They looked like two more small dogs.

I pressed my face closer to the crack just as the door swung open. The shapes I'd seen were Mrs. Lawton's feet in a pair of fuzzy slippers. I craned my neck and looked up at her from where I lay on the porch.

She looked back down at me with a shocked expression on her face.

"Goodness gracious," she said. "Are you all right, young man? Let me help you up." She bent down and offered me a hand. "It's a wonder more people don't pass out when it gets this hot."

"No, Mrs. Lawton," I said, standing up. "I'm really okay. I was just lying down."

"Nonsense," she said. "Come right inside, and I'll fix you a cold drink. You'll feel better in no time."

"No, ma'am," I protested. "I just came over to—" But her tiny shape was already shuffling down the dark hallway away from me.

I stood there a moment wondering what to do. Just then I remembered I still had the brass 2 in my hand. I glanced up at the door where the missing number should have been. I sighed. I looked into the house, but I couldn't see Mrs. Lawton anymore. I slipped the brass number into my pocket, stepped inside, and pulled the door shut behind me.

I'd never been inside Mrs. Lawton's house before. It was dimly lit and smelled a little dusty. A bunch of narrow doorways opened off the hallway, and I had no idea where Mrs. Lawton had gone. I started down the hallway, glancing into each room as I went. The rooms were small and oddly shaped, each with flowered wallpaper and antiques. The walls were cluttered with framed pictures. It was even hotter inside the house than out, and there was no sign of Mrs. Lawton.

"Hello?" I called. "Mrs. Lawton?"

In a few minutes, I was sitting in an uncomfortable antique chair sipping lemonade with a tiny Pekingese dog sniffing at my shoes. Mrs. Lawton spoke to my mom on a cordless phone she'd brought in from the kitchen. The phone seemed out of place in this old house.

"... I opened the door and found him passed out on the front porch," Mrs. Lawton said into the phone. "He seems to be doing fine now."

I winced, imagining Mom on the other end of the line.

"Yes, of course you can talk to him." Mrs. Lawton held the phone out to me.

I took it and put it to my ear. "Willie," Mom said, "what's going on over there?" The tone of her voice seemed more irritated than concerned. I guess I have a history of this sort of thing. Mom's gotten more than a few bizarre phone calls about me.

"It's kind of hard to explain," I told her. I could feel Mrs. Lawton watching me. "Both of us are fine, though. Everything's okay."

"You're sure?" Mom asked. "You haven't *done* anything to the poor woman have you?"

"Of course not," I said. "Everything's fine here. I'll be back home in a few minutes." I pressed the button that hung up the phone, and Mrs. Lawton took it back in the kitchen.

"You have to remember not to exert yourself on such a hot day," Mrs. Lawton told me from the other room. "I'm surprised I don't faint myself sometimes."

When she came back in the parlor, she lifted her hair to let the air reach her neck. The light in her parlor was dim, but I could tell she was weary with the heat—and here I'd come sending her into a panic and making her fetch me lemonade.

"Don't you have any fans you could use?" I asked her.

"Just the one," she told me. "It's upstairs in my bedroom."

"You could cool this place down a lot if you'd cross-ventilate," I told her. "Look, we've got a few big fans out in the garage that we haven't used since my dad put air conditioning in the hobby shop. If I got them, I bet we could cool this place down fast."

"Oh, you shouldn't be exerting yourself after your fainting spell."

I grinned. "I feel pretty good, actually," I told her. "And this will be a way for me to pay you back for your hospitality."

Our garage was as hot as Mrs. Lawton's house. The four big steel fans were crowded in a back corner, and by the time I'd wrestled them free, I was covered with dust, cobwebs, and sweat. I got some rags and started dusting them off.

"Willie," Mom called from inside the house. "Phone call."

It had to be either Felix or Samantha, my two best friends. Maybe I could get one of them to help me move the fans down the street to Mrs. Lawton's.

I went inside the house and headed to the kitchen. When Mom saw me come in, she grinned. I looked down at my T-shirt. It was covered with dust and streaked with black oil from the fans. I thought she'd get mad since it was a new shirt, but she just smiled as she handed me the phone. I think she was glad to see me doing something other than lying on the sofa, especially since I was helping Mrs. Lawton.

"Hello?" I said into the phone.

"Dude," Felix said. "Were you watching the news? Did you see that two-headed collie?"

"No, Felix," I said dryly. "I have more important things to do than sit around all day watching television." I winked at Mom. She grinned, shook her head, and headed out the swinging kitchen door.

"It was freaky," Felix said. "It had this second head that stuck out from the side of its neck. It could even bark."

"You called to tell me about a two-headed dog?" I said. "Sounds like someone needs to get a life."

"Actually, I was just calling to see what you were doing," Felix said. "Want to come over and play video games or something?"

"How about you come help me?" I said. "I'm taking some things down the street to a neighbor, and I could use some help. They're pretty heavy."

There were a few seconds of silence on the other end of the phone. "You mean like go outside?" Felix said.

"No, Felix," I told him. "I've dug an underground tunnel, just so you won't have to go outside."

"Don't get snippy, Willie," Felix said. "I was just asking. Do you want my help or not?"

"Yes, I want your help. Why don't you swing by Sam's house and see if she can come too?"

"No dice," Felix said. "She went out to her aunt's farm and picked up a bunch of puppies this morning."

"Puppies?" I said.

"You know: little dogs," Felix said, as though I might not know. "Now she's got to fix up the back yard for them."

"What's she going to do with a bunch of puppies?"

"She's going to make a fur coat out of them," Felix said. "How am I supposed to know? Look, are we going to do something or not?"

"Okay, okay," I said. "Get on over here. We've got an old lady to rescue."

There was a few seconds' pause. "Whatever you say, Willie," Felix said and hung up the phone.

Puppy Love

Felix pretended to be very put out at having to help me carry the fans, but he worked hard, and in less than an hour, we'd hauled them up on Mrs. Lawton's porch. I rang the doorbell. Again it took a few minutes for Mrs. Lawton to answer.

Inside, Felix and I looked around the whole house, trying to come up with a plan. It was a big house, full of lots of tiny rooms and odd corners. It would be hard to get the air flowing smoothly with only four fans. We wouldn't be able to cool down the whole house, but if we closed off some of the rooms, we thought we could keep the main parts of the house ventilated enough to be comfortable.

Felix went upstairs to close some doors, and I went down the main hallway with Mrs. Lawton, closing off some of the downstairs rooms. Each room was crowded with antique furniture, paintings and knick-knacks, but the most striking thing about the house was all the photographs. Every desk, table, and mantle was covered with framed photos. Most of them were inscribed.

As I came back up the hallway, a particular photo on a side table next to the stairs caught my eye. It was a photo of a much younger Mrs. Lawton with another woman and two men. The photo was taken in a big room with a high ceiling. One of the men had a mustache. The other man looked strangely familiar. He had black hair and was wearing a suit and tie. Where had I seen him before? I picked up the photo and squinted at it. Something was written in the lower corner with a black pen, but I couldn't make out much of the writing, and the signature was just a scribble.

"Who's the man in this photo?" I asked, turning the frame so Mrs. Lawton could see it.

She smiled wistfully. "That's my late husband, Wendell," she said. "Wasn't he a handsome man? I absolutely hated the mustache though. I eventually got him to shave it off."

"No," I said. "I meant who is the other guy? Haven't I seen him before?"

Mrs. Lawton looked at me like she thought I was pulling her leg. Just then Felix came down the stairs. "Really?" she said. "You don't know who that is?"

I shrugged. I felt a little embarrassed. She looked at Felix.

"How about you, Felix?" she asked, holding the photo out to him. "Do you know who this man is?"

Felix looked at the photo, then looked up at Mrs. Lawton suddenly, like he was shocked. "What were you doing with President Nixon?" he asked.

Of course! I thought. It was Richard Nixon. I *knew* I'd seen him before; I just didn't expect him to be famous. I was trying to think of someone who lived in Glenfield.

"Dick and Pat were our good friends," she said. "In those days, we spent a lot of time at the White House."

I looked around at more of the photos. A lot of them had people I sort of recognized. I picked up another frame. The photo showed a bald man at a table, drawing something on a piece of paper. "Who's this?" I asked.

She glanced at the photo. "That's Pablo Picasso, a famous artist. I only met him that one time, but he was a very nice man. He did a sketch of me. It's hanging in the front room."

I was stunned. "A famous artist drew a picture of you?" I sputtered. "You have a real Picasso in your house? It must be worth millions!"

"Nonsense," she said. "It was just a quick sketch. He did it while I was taking his picture."

Felix was peering at every picture in the room now. He nudged me and pointed to a photo on the wall. It was a photo of Mrs. Lawton, much younger,

standing beside a man with white hair and a bushy
white beard. There were mountains and snow in the
background.

"Wow," I said. "You even knew Santa Claus."

Mrs. Lawton laughed. "That's Ernest Hemingway," she said. "That was taken at his ranch in Idaho."

"We read his book, *The Old Man and the Sea*, in
English class," Felix said. "How did you get to meet so
many famous people?"

Mrs. Lawton smiled and looked at the ground.
"Well, believe it or not," she said, "I was a little bit
famous myself."

"Really?" I said. "Who were you?"

"I was Eudora Lawton," she teased. "What a silly
question."

"I meant, what did you do to be famous?"

"I was a photographer," she said. "I worked for
the army when I was 19, taking photos during World
War II. After that I worked for *Life* magazine. Then I
did a lot of portraits. It seemed like everyone wanted
to be photographed by Eudora Lawton in those days."

After looking at a few more pictures, Felix and I
got back to work. We set up one fan in front of the
back screen door so it sucked cool air in from the
shady backyard. Another fan in the kitchen doorway
moved the cool air through the parlor. We placed the
third fan at the top of the stairs to suck the air up to
the second floor and the last fan in Mrs. Lawton's bedroom window to blow the air out. We turned all the

fans on, and Mrs. Lawton brought us lemonade in the parlor. With all the fans going, it was hard to hear each other talk, but in just a few minutes we could feel the air start to cool. It wasn't as good as air conditioning, but it made a big difference. I just sat there smiling, sipping lemonade and listening to Felix and Mrs. Lawton talk about all the famous people Mrs. Lawton knew. Felix and I had done a pretty good deed.

When Felix and I left Mrs. Lawton's house, we still had more than an hour until dinner time, and an hour after that until the sun went down. It was still hot, but there was a hint of a breeze now, and the afternoon heat was beginning to fade. We stood on the sidewalk in front of Mrs. Lawton's house, not sure what to do.

"I dropped off a roll of film at Shaw's Photo and Framing yesterday," Felix said. "He had a signed photo of Mark McGwire up on the wall. You wouldn't believe how much he was asking for it."

"So?" I asked. Sometimes it took Felix a while to get to the point.

"Well, can you imagine how much all those signed photos in Mrs. Lawton's house are worth?" Felix said.

He glanced over his shoulder at the old house. "She said she had boxes full of letters too. And that Picasso sketch. There must be a million dollars worth of collectibles in that old house."

"Could be," I said.

"You think she'd sell any of them?" Felix asked. "I'm looking for a good investment. I've got to make some money."

"You've got like three hundred dollars saved up," I pointed out. "What do you want with more money?"

"Church camp is coming up in a couple of weeks," Felix told me. "I have to pay my own way this year. I've *got* to make some money. How much do you think she'd want for that Ernest Hemingway?"

"Forget it," I told him. "She's not going to sell it. That stuff means a lot to her. There are more important things in life than money."

Felix sighed and looked both ways down the street.

"Want to come over and watch TV?" I asked.

Felix rubbed the back of his neck. "Nah," he said, "I've been watching TV all week." He pulled his T-shirt away from his body, as though the sweat was making it stick. "How about we go over to Sam's house and look at the puppies? Maybe one of them has two heads."

"Two heads?" I said. "Don't you think that's the sort of detail she'd have mentioned when you had her on the phone?"

"I didn't ask, and she didn't say," Felix said. He took off his glasses and rubbed his eyes. "Well let's go look at them anyway," he said. "It's got to be better than watching TV."

When we got to Sam's house, we went up to the front door and rang the bell. We heard Sam's voice call out from around the side of the house. "Is that ooo guys?" Sam said. Her voice sounded muffled and strange. I looked at Felix. He shrugged. "I'm around ack," Sam called. "Umm to the side gate."

Felix and I walked across the driveway to the side gate. Sam stood looking over the gate at us. She held a tiny puppy on one arm and a big bag of Puppy Chow under the other. She held a thick book in her teeth. I read the title: *A Breeder's Guide to Golden Retrievers*.

"Umm on in," she told us. I reached over the fence and unlatched the gate. I pushed it open so Felix could pass through and then closed it behind me. Sam looked a little frazzled. She had grass stains on the knees of her jeans and leaves stuck in her hair. The puppy she held squirmed suddenly, and she nearly dropped the bag of puppy food.

"Let's see these puppies," Felix said, heading toward the backyard.

Sam glared at him. "Ow about elping me ith this stuff?" Sam tried to ask around the book in her teeth.

"Sorry," Felix said, "I can't understand you with that book in your mouth." He disappeared around the back of the house.

I laughed and took the book from Sam's teeth.

"Do you *believe* that guy?" she said to me. "I hope they eat you alive," she yelled after him.

I took the bag of dog food from Sam and followed her around to the backyard. When we turned the corner, I saw a tumble of blonde puppies growling and pouncing and rolling around in play. The yard was a mess. Sam had built a small pen in a shady corner with chicken wire, but it was flattened and trampled into the grass. The puppies' water bowl had been capsized, and the grass was torn up and muddy where the water had puddled. Leaves, twigs, stones, and scraps of trash littered Mrs. Stewart's usually immaculate backyard. A few flower pots were knocked over. One pup was chewing on a cloth gardener's glove.

"I can't keep them in," Sam said. "They're like a bunch of little dog Houdinis. They keep tearing up my mom's plants. She's going to kill me."

Felix knelt in the grass and three of the puppies started jumping on him and tugging at his clothes.

"What are you doing with all these pups?" I asked Sam.

"I got them from my Aunt Kathy. She breeds golden retrievers on her farm. This litter is just a month or so old."

"But why are they *here*?"

"Aunt Kathy figured it would be easier for me to sell them here in town than for her to sell them way out in the country. We're splitting the money."

I looked down to find a tiny puppy tugging at my shoelace. The shoelace came loose and the pup tumbled backwards into one of Mrs. Stewart's flower beds. When he climbed back out, I bent down and offered him my hand. He pounced on it and nipped at it with his sharp little teeth. It reminded me of how much fun Sadie, my cocker spaniel, was when she was a pup.

"They're so cute," I said. "How much are you asking for them?" I picked up the pup and held him under my chin. His fur was soft and warm on my neck.

"Three hundred dollars for the boys," Sam told me. "Three fifty for the girls."

My mouth dropped open. "Are you serious?" I held the tiny pup at arm's length and looked him over. "Three hundred bucks for this little pipsqueak? He wouldn't make a decent guinea pig."

"Are you kidding?" Sam asked. "They're a bargain. At Luigi's Pet Shop, they'd go for twice that."

She was right. I'd once had a job at Luigi's Pet Shop in the Glenfield Mall, and puppies *were* incredibly expensive. I looked down at the pup in my hands. "So you get at least a hundred and fifty bucks for each of these little guys?"

"Yeah," she said.

I glanced over at Felix. He was lying on his back on the ground now. Six or seven puppies were swarming all over him, licking his face and tugging at his T-shirt. "Somebody help me," he shouted dramatically. "No, leave me here. I'm done for. Save your own lives."

Sam shook her head and grinned.

"Nine pups at a hundred and fifty." I squinted up at the clouds and did the math in my head. "That's thirteen hundred and fifty dollars!"

Felix propped himself up on one elbow, suddenly attentive. "You're going to make over thirteen hundred dollars on these little rats?"

"Yeah," Sam said. "But I have to pay for their food and for the ad in the paper. And I have to take care of them until they all sell. I'm *earning* that money."

"You need any investors?" Felix wanted to know. "I need to make some quick money, and I could invest a couple hundred dollars."

"I've got everything covered," Sam told him. "If you've got a couple hundred dollars, why do you need to make some quick money?"

"Camp," Felix said. "My parents paid to fix my telescope, so if I'm going to camp, I have to pay my own way this year."

"That's right," I told her. "We've got church camp in a couple of weeks. You're going to have to sell these dogs pretty quick. You sure you can do it?"

"I guess I'll have to," she said. "But *look* at them. They're so cute. Who could resist?"

I looked down at the pup cupped in my hands again. He blinked up at me. He had an odd expression on his face. It was almost like he was trying to smile at me. "Will you look at the face he's making?" I said. "I think he likes me."

"Sounds like I might have my first sale," Sam said. "Like I said: Who can resist a puppy?"

The puppy was still looking up at me with that expression on his face when I noticed that my hand was filled with a warm liquid. So *that's* what the face he was making meant!

"Oh, gross!" I quickly set him down on the lawn and shook my dripping hands. "That's totally sick," I said.

Sam started laughing and ran to get the garden hose.

"I think *I* can resist a puppy," I told her as she held the hose out to me so I could wash my hands.

Once my hands were clean, I helped Sam set up her chicken wire pen again. We twisted the loose ends of the chicken wire together so it made a big circle. We made the pen as secure as we could, and then we chased down every loose puppy and put them back where they belonged.

We both knew it wouldn't be for long.

Dog Gone

All an inventor really needs is a problem that asks to be solved. People who lived far away from each other needed to talk, so Alexander Graham Bell invented the telephone. People got tired of bumping into furniture in the dark, so Thomas Edison invented the light bulb. Once people could stay up late because of Edison's light bulbs, they needed something to do, so Guglielmo Marconi invented the radio. Well, Sam had a bunch of puppies that needed to be kept inside a puppy-proof enclosure. So I, Willie Plummet, invented the Puppy Corral.

After dinner, when the garage had cooled down a bit, I went out to see what I could find to work with. I found a lot of old PVC piping Dad had used last spring when he put in our sprinklers. I set about forming it into a large rectangular frame. Next I fitted it with chicken wire and loops of canvas so it could be secured to the ground with tent stakes. On one side I attached a long plastic planter that could be filled with Puppy Chow, like a feeding trough. On the opposite side, I attached a water dish that couldn't be turned upside down.

When I was done, I stepped back to look at it. It seemed sturdy and strong enough. They'd *really* have to be puppy Houdinis to escape from the Puppy Corral! And it was big enough to hold all nine pups!

It was then that I discovered the problem. The Puppy Corral took up half the garage floor. How was I going to move it over to Sam's house? It was even too big to fit in the back of my big brother Orville's pickup—*if* I could talk him into helping. I'd have to take the whole thing apart, get Orville to help me move it, and assemble it again in Sam's backyard.

Orville! He was the typical high school big brother. He made Godzilla look cooperative. There was no way he'd help me unless he was forced to. I knew better than to even bother asking him.

I opened the door into the house. "Mom," I called from the garage. "Mom, I want to show you something."

In a few seconds Mom appeared in the doorway drying her hands on a dishtowel. "What is it, Willie?"

"It's my latest invention," I told her. I stepped aside so she could see the Puppy Corral. "It's to keep Sam's puppies from destroying Mrs. Stewart's garden." I walked around the corral, pointing out its special features and emphasizing how helpful it would be for Sam and her mother. Then I sighed dramatically. "Now all I've got to do is find a way to get it over to Sam's house," I said. "It'll take me all day if I carry the parts over on foot."

"Well, can't Orville drop you off on his way to work tomorrow?" Mom suggested.

"Hey, that's a great idea," I told her, as if it had never occurred to me. "But I know he'll say no as soon as I ask him." I looked dejectedly down at the floor.

"Well, let me ask him," Mom said.

"Would you, Mom?" I said excitedly. "Would you, really?"

Poor Orville. He was no match for Willie Plummet!

I called Sam to tell her I'd be over in the morning with the Puppy Corral.

By the time I'd taken my invention apart, it was time for bed. I sat on the edge of my bed and pulled off my shorts. When I did, something clanked to the floor. It was a big brass 2. I'd forgotten to give it to Mrs. Lawton. I sighed. I'd have to go by her place tomorrow and put it back up on her door frame again.

At least it would give me a chance to see how well our ventilation job had worked overnight.

The next morning I slipped the brass 2 into the pocket of my shorts and went downstairs to breakfast. Dad had already left to open the hobby shop for the day, so only Orville, Mom, and my big sister Amanda were at the breakfast table when I got there. I sat down across from Orville and he glared at me. Mom had obviously told him he'd be helping me take the Puppy Corral over to Sam's house.

"Let me warm up some pancakes for you, Willie," Mom said. She got up from her place at the table and went through the swinging door into the kitchen.

"That junk of yours had better be in the back of my pickup in 10 minutes," Orville said, not loud enough for Mom to hear in the kitchen, "or it's getting left behind."

I leaned forward and gave him my most annoying grin. "Mom said you *had* to drop me off at Sam's house," I reminded him smugly.

"*Dad* said I had to be at work by 9:00, smart guy," Orville said.

I glanced up at the kitchen clock: 8:30. *Yikes!*

I jumped up from the table and ran out to the garage. In five minutes, I'd loaded all the parts of the Puppy Corral onto the back of Orville's pickup. My bare knees felt bruised and banged up from kneeling on the garage floor.

I knew I'd be on my knees most of the morning assembling the Puppy Corral in Sam's backyard, so I used my last few minutes to dash upstairs and change from shorts into a new pair of jeans. They felt a little stiff, but it was better than wearing shorts.

I got downstairs just as Orville slammed the front door. I grabbed the three pancakes Mom had put at my place at the table and dashed out the front door just as Orville rolled down the driveway in his pickup.

When Orville pulled over to the curb in front of Sam's house I unbuckled my seat belt and dusted pancake crumbs from the front of my T-shirt. I waited for Orville to turn off the engine. He hadn't spoken a word to me since we'd left the breakfast table.

After a few seconds, he looked over at me. "Well?" he said.

"Well what?"

"Aren't you going to get out?"

"I thought you were going to help me."

"You need help getting out of the truck?" he said. "You want me to carry you to the curb or something?"

"No," I said. "Help with the stuff in back. Mom said you were supposed to drop the Puppy Corral off at Sam's house."

"No," Orville corrected me. "She told me to drop *you* off at Sam's house. What happens to your stupid puppy prison is your business. Now get out of my truck."

I sighed and opened the door. The heat hit me as soon as I stepped down onto the asphalt.

"At least help me get it out of the truck," I asked him.

"This truck is leaving in 15 seconds," Orville informed me, "and whatever's left in it is going with me."

I sighed and walked around the back of the truck. I pulled the tailgate open and started piling the parts of the Puppy Corral on the sidewalk in front of Sam's house.

Orville revved up his engine as I unloaded the last few pieces. As soon as I slammed the tailgate shut, he took off down the street. His brake lights came on as he turned the corner, and he was out of sight. Big brothers!

I picked up one section of the Puppy Corral and took it to Sam's side fence. I reached over and unlatched the gate. I carefully carried the first section of the corral through and closed the gate behind me. When I got to the backyard, Sam was filling a water dish from the garden hose. Three of the puppies were tumbling around her feet in a rambunctious fight. One of them gave a pained squeal as another bit its ear.

"Benny," Sam scolded. "Not so rough. You hurt Sky."

Sam looked up from what she was doing. "Oh, hi, Willie," she said. "You're just in time. We were about to leave."

"Your puppies all have names now?" I asked.

"Yeah," Sam said. "They're really growing on me."

I looked around at the puppies in the yard. They all looked the same to me. "You can tell them apart?"

"Of course," she said.

"Which one's this?" I quizzed her, looking down at the tiny pup sniffing at my heels.

"Shawna," she said. "She's got a darker coat and that wrinkle on her forehead."

I looked down at the pup and then at a few of the others. They all looked identical. "If you say so," I said.

I set the first section of the Puppy Corral in the shade of one of Mrs. Stewart's maple trees.

"It that your new invention?" Sam asked.

"Part of it," I said. "The rest is out front."

"You look hot," she said. "I'm making iced tea. Want some before I take off?"

"That would be great," I said. "I'll be right in when I get the rest of it back here."

When all the parts of the corral were stacked in the backyard, I went to the sliding glass door and pulled it open. Sam was at the kitchen sink stirring a pitcher of iced tea. She poured me a glass.

"I really appreciate you making the corral for me," she said. "I already owe Mom about 30 dollars in damages. Those little guys are destructive."

"No sweat," I told her. "With me around, your puppies are as safe as if they were in ... well ... a *safe*."

I paused. The image didn't quite say what I wanted it to say. "But with holes in the safe so they could breathe," I rubbed the back of my neck. "And food and water and stuff." Fortunately, Sam didn't seem to be listening.

"I wish I could stay and help you set it up," Sam said as she rinsed out her iced tea glass and set it in the sink. "But this is the only time Mom can drop me off at the *Glenfield Gazette* to put an ad in tomorrow's paper."

"It's okay," I said. "Felix will be here any moment. We'll have it put together in no time. It's a piece of cake to assemble."

"Sam!" Mrs. Stewart called from the front room. "We'd better get on the road now. I've got a lot of errands to run before your father gets home."

"I'll be right there," Sam called back. She went to the glass door and looked out at the backyard. "What did you do with them?" Sam asked.

"With what?"

"The pups," she said.

"Don't worry about the pups," I told her. "I'll take good care of them."

"Yeah, but where are they?"

I stood beside her at the sliding glass door and looked out. Two of the puppies were playing on the lawn and one was napping under Mrs. Stewart's wheelbarrow. The air shimmered with heat. "They're probably back in the bushes enjoying the shade," I said. "Don't give it a thought. They're in good hands."

Mrs. Stewart appeared in the kitchen doorway jingling her keys impatiently. "Let's go," she said.

When I finished the iced tea, I was alone in the house. I rinsed out my glass and put it in the sink next to Sam's. Then I went out in the backyard and set to assembling the Puppy Corral. At first, a couple of the puppies kept barking and nipping at my clothes, but after a while, they left me alone. Even though it was hot, I had a good time. I was immersed in my work, and it felt good to be doing another good deed.

By the time I was done assembling the corral, I was hot and thirsty. I couldn't wait to pour myself another glass of iced tea. It was a reward I deserved. I twisted the piece of plastic piping in place and straightened up. My knees and back ached a little. I was glad I was wearing jeans.

I stepped back and looked at the corral, neatly constructed and staked down under the shade of Mrs. Stewart's maple tree. It was really something to see. It looked like a miniature piece of farm equipment. All it needed was some water in the water dish and some food in the feeding trough. I felt a real sense of accomplishment. It's moments like this that an inventor lives for.

I stretched and turned to look for the puppies. I couldn't see a single one.

I got down on my hand and knees and peeked under the bushes. "Here, puppies," I sang. "Nice puppies." I got down as low as I could. There were no puppies in the bushes.

I looked along the back fence and behind a row of planters. No puppies. I walked down along the side of the house. I looked behind the trash cans. I looked around the shrubs. I looked behind the open gate.

Open gate?

"*Ahhhhhh*," I screamed, falling to my knees and holding the sides of my head. I'd left the side gate open! The puppies were gone!

Dog Catcher

By the time Felix turned the corner onto Sam's street, I was frantic. After half an hour of searching, I'd only found two of the pups and put them safely in the finished corral. It was hot, exhausting work, and I was drenched in sweat. Felix wobbled toward me on his bike.

"Am I glad to see you!" I shouted when he got close enough to hear. "I'm in big trouble. I let them all loose. Sam's going to kill me."

"What are you talking about?"

"The puppies," I said as Felix wobbled to a stop in front of me. "I left the gate open. They're all gone. If they're not all in the Puppy Corral when Sam gets home, I'm ... I'm ..." In my frantic state, I couldn't think of how to finish the sentence.

"In the doghouse?" Felix ventured. He started laughing at his own dumb joke. It was just like Felix to make a joke when my world was falling apart.

"Not funny," I said angrily. "Not funny at all. I've lost about 50 thousand dollars worth of puppies, and you're making jokes."

Felix got off his bike and rolled it up Sam's driveway. "I always thought we had a good arrangement here," Felix said. "You provide the disasters, and I provide the comic relief."

"Fine," I growled. "Just save the comedy until the disaster is over. Come on. We've got puppies to find."

Felix dumped his bike in Sam's driveway, and we took off down the street hunting for the puppies. I walked on one side of the street and Felix on the other so we could check around the houses on both sides.

"Here, Shawna! Here, Sky!" I called.

"Here, Abbott! Here, Costello!" Felix called from the opposite sidewalk.

I stopped walking and glared over at him. "What are you doing?"

"I'm calling the puppies," Felix said. He stopped walking too. He looked across at me, a little bewildered.

"Those aren't their names."

"What do they care?" Felix said. "They don't even know their names. They're puppies."

He had a point, but I was in no mood to humor him. "Use their real names," I told him. "This is no time to be goofing around."

"Fine. Whatever," Felix said, rubbing the back of his neck. "Tell me their real names."

I didn't answer him. I started walking again. Felix was really ticking me off.

"Well?" he called from across the street.

"I don't know their names," I yelled across at him.

"Then what are you yelling at me for?" Felix shouted back.

"I may not know their names," I shouted back, practically foaming at the mouth. "But, I know they're not named Abbott and Costello!"

Felix grinned suddenly.

"What are you grinning at?" I demanded.

"I just found Abbott and Costello," Felix said. "They're under that minivan."

The van was parked in a driveway on my side of the street. I ran over, got down on my knees and looked under. One puppy was on its back and the other was growling and pouncing and biting like a wild animal in a nature film. Both of them were wagging their tails.

I laid on my back and reached under to get them, but they scooted away from me. They seemed to think this was some sort of game. I crawled completely under the van, but each time I got within reach of them they scooted away from me. Being so small, they could maneuver a lot better than I could.

"Don't just stand there, Felix," I called from under the minivan. "*Do* something." I felt something drip on the side of my face. I rubbed my cheek and looked at my hand. It was covered with black grease.

"What do you want me to do?"

"Get under here and help me corner these guys."

There was a few seconds of silence. "Only if you apologize," Felix said.

"For what?"

"For yelling at me."

I was about to yell at him again, but instead I bumped my head on the bottom of the van. *Owwwwww*. I rested my cheek on the warm driveway a moment. My head was throbbing. It was only 10:00 in the morning. How did everything manage to get so messed up so early in the day?

"Okay, okay," I sighed. "I'm sorry I yelled at you. You can call them Abbott and Costello. You can call them Laurel and Hardy if you want. You can call them anything. Just get under here."

"Even Larry, Moe, and Curly?" Felix said, crawling under the far side of the van.

"There's only two of them," I pointed out.

Felix reached for the puppies. They backed toward me, and I caught one of them by the tail. Felix grabbed the other. We scrambled out from under the van.

Felix held his puppy up close to his face. "*Ow, wise guy, eh?*" he said, trying to sound like one of the Three Stooges. Felix's clothes and hair were streaked with grease. I laughed at him. I couldn't help it. It was such a relief to find even just two more of the puppies. That was 600 dollars I didn't owe Sam. "You should see yourself," I told him. "You look pretty funny."

"Don't have to see myself," he said. "I'm having enough fun looking at you."

I glanced down at my own T-shirt. It was stained even worse than his, and it had a tear on one shoulder. My hands and arms were streaked with black motor oil. The pup, however, was perfectly clean. Felix just stood there grinning at me. I was in deep trouble, but I started laughing anyway.

When we got back to Sam's house, we put the two pups in the Puppy Corral with the two I'd already found. I made sure we closed the gate when we went out to look for the rest.

"How many pups did she have anyway?" Felix asked as we walked across Sam's front lawn to the sidewalk.

"Nine," I told him.

"You sure?"

"Sure I'm sure," I told him.

I stopped at the sidewalk and looked up and down the street, wondering what to do next. "Maybe if we split up, we could cover more ground," I suggested.

Felix shrugged. "Makes sense to me," he said.

"You go that way," I told him. "I'll go this way."

Felix just stood there. "Aren't we going to synchronize our watches or something?"

I sighed. "Sure, Felix," I said, trying not to sound exasperated. "We can synchronize our watches." I glanced down at my wristwatch. "What time do you have?"

"I don't actually *have* a watch," Felix said. "You think I could borrow yours?"

I walked away from him. "You're not funny, Felix," I said loud enough for him to hear. "You think you're funny, but you're not."

I walked a couple of blocks, looking down the sides of houses and behind bushes. Each time I came to a corner, I stood debating with myself which direction to go. None of them seemed any more likely than the others. The sun was high in the sky now. It wasn't as hot as yesterday, but it was still a horrible day to be out looking for puppies. I wondered how Mrs. Lawton was doing in her hot, old house.

I came to a corner and glanced down the street. There was a big commotion of little kids. They were in someone's front yard, running around in circles and laughing. I stopped a moment and listened. Amid all the laughter and shouting, I heard a couple of high-pitched barks. I took off running toward them.

When I got closer, I saw the little puppy they were chasing. It ran in circles while the children ran away from it in mock terror. The pup stopped suddenly, barked twice, and took off running again. It wagged its tail so frantically it could barely stay on its feet.

Maybe I forgot how big I was. Maybe I shouted too loud. But when I came barreling down the street yelling, "Grab that puppy!" all the little kids scattered, terrified. The puppy took off running too, right under someone's side fence, into their backyard.

I ran around to the front of the house and rang the doorbell. I waited and rang again, but there was no answer. There was nothing I could do. I had no choice in the matter. I'd have to climb the fence into the backyard. I knew it was trespassing, but this was an emergency. I jogged back around to where the puppy had disappeared under the fence.

The fence was about six feet tall and made out of white boards. I was pretty sure I could make it over.

"Hey, Mister," a voice said. One of the little kids peeked over the hood of a car parked in the next driveway. "Is that your dog?"

"Yeah," I told him. "Sort of. He ran away, and I've got to get him back."

The kid ducked behind the car a moment. I heard him whisper to some other kid hiding back there. His head peeked over the car again. "Mr. Beanan said we shouldn't climb on his fence," the kid told me.

"It's okay," I said. "It's an emergency. I'll be careful." I grabbed the top of one of the white boards and scrambled up so I was straddling the fence.

"Mr. Beanan said we shouldn't climb on his fence until the paint dries," the kid said.

Paint? I looked down at my palms. Each one had a white streak across it. I glanced down at my new jeans. They were streaked with white paint. I sighed and slapped one hand on my forehead before I remembered the paint on my palm. I could hear the kids giggling behind the parked car.

"Thanks for the warning, kid," I told him. I hopped down on the other side of the fence.

It took me a few minutes to corner the puppy in the backyard against the fence, but I eventually got him in hand and came back along the side of the fence where I'd climbed over.

It looked like Mr. Beanan had run out of paint; only half of the side fence was painted. He was probably out buying more paint right now. If I hopped over the unpainted half of the fence into his neighbor's yard, I could come along the side of his neighbor's house and get back out front. I climbed up on a tree stump and looked over the fence with the puppy under one arm. The neighbor's backyard was empty.

"Hello?" I called. "Anyone home?" Nothing stirred on the other side of the fence.

I looked down at the puppy under my arm. "What do you think?" I asked. "Should we go for it?"

If the puppy had any objections, he didn't say anything.

From the tree stump, I had no trouble hopping up on top of the fence. I paused there a moment, surveying the neighbor's yard. The neighbor had a gate at the side of his house, so I wouldn't even have to climb over to get back out front. To make things even easier, there was a large wooden crate turned on its side, just below where I was perched on the fence. All I had to do was hop down on top of the crate and let myself out by the side gate.

"Hang on," I told the puppy. I jumped down on top of the crate with a loud thud. I heard a deep bark and a growl. I felt the sound resonate in the wooden crate beneath me. It wasn't a crate; it was a doghouse!

I leaped off the top of the doghouse and sprinted along the side of the house toward the gate. I grabbed the rusty latch on the gate and made the mistake of glancing behind me. A huge slobbering bulldog charged out of the doghouse and rocketed down the side of the house in my direction.

Forget the gate! I leapt up on the fence and pulled myself up with one arm, just as the bulldog snapped at my heels. I paused, perched on top of the fence, my heart pounding. The bulldog jumped up at me and flung its muscular body against the fence with a thud. My nerves were frazzled.

"Hey, Mister," a voice said. I looked down from where I sat clinging to the fence. The two little kids had come out from behind the car and were standing in the driveway. "I have a dog too," the one kid said. "It's a bulldog. It's pretty mean."

"Thanks for the warning," I told him again.

When I got back to Sam's backyard, I found Felix lying in the Puppy Corral on his back while the recovered puppies swarmed all over him. He was squirming and giggling. His glasses lay on the grass beside him. He didn't see me coming.

"What do you think you're doing?" I shouted.

Felix jumped. He sat up, felt on the ground beside him for his glasses and put them on. "I was just taking a break," he said. "I just got here. Honest."

I leaned over the wall of the corral and set the puppy I'd just found in among the others. I counted them. There were seven now. Felix must have found two more, but I still wanted to yell at him. "We've got work to do," I told him. "Get out of there and start looking for the other two."

Felix stood up sheepishly and dusted off his pants.

"What happened to you?" he said.

I looked down at my clothes. They were covered with streaks of white paint. "Nothing," I told him coolly. "Nothing happened to me. Now get back out there and find the last two puppies."

It felt like I'd been walking for hours under the hot sun. I'd wandered up and down every street in Sam's neighborhood without any sign of a puppy. My legs were sticky and itchy in my new jeans. I wished I'd kept my shorts on. I glanced at my watch. It was nearly noon. Sam could be home any minute. I wiped the sweat off my forehead with my arm.

The thought crossed my mind that Felix might have found the last two puppies already, and he might be waiting back at Sam's house for me right now. I really wanted to turn around and head back, but there was no way to know. I decided I'd walk for 15 more minutes, and, if nothing turned up, I'd head back and face Sam with or without the last two puppies. I'd just have to take it like a man.

About 10 minutes later, I found myself at the park on Pickett Avenue. It wasn't very big. It just had a small duck pond, a gazebo, and a few benches under the trees.

It didn't have a playground, and there wasn't enough room for a decent game of football or soccer, so none of the kids in the neighborhood played there. It was usually only used by old people who would come there to feed the ducks or play checkers. It was so hot today, none of the old people were around. I was the only person there.

I thought with it being so hot, maybe the dogs would be attracted to the duck pond, so I headed down the cracked pathway that led to the water. The lawns were brown and full of crabgrass. The white paint on the gazebo was cracked and peeling, and the benches needed repair. There were no flowers in the weedy flower beds.

I came to the top of a little hill, and suddenly I could see the duck pond. The water level was lower than I'd ever seen it. A few ducks floated on the glittering surface. I shaded my eyes with my hand and squinted. Sure enough, there was a puppy down at the edge of the water splashing around.

I took off running. This puppy was not going to escape! When I got close to the pond I slowed down. The half-submerged puppy was looking out over the water at the ducks. It growled at them and barked twice. That was just the distraction I needed. I tiptoed down the steep bank of the pond to the water's edge. The puppy had no idea I was there. It barked at the ducks again and wagged its tail.

I pounced into the shallow water with both feet and snatched up the unsuspecting pup. As I straightened up, one of my feet twisted sideways in the slippery mud. I tried to keep my balance, but my hands were busy trying to keep my grip on a damp, squirming pup. I thrashed around in the shallow water a moment, trying to keep my balance, then both feet shot out from under me. The next thing I knew, I was lying on my back in the mud, holding a puppy straight up in the air.

Muddy pond water lapped at my ears, and I was completely submerged up to my navel. I lay there a few seconds looking up at the sky and the dripping puppy. In an odd way it was a serene moment. I felt the cool water seeping into my jeans. The puppy looked down at me and wagged his tail.

I knew that by the time I got back to Sam's house I'd feel like a glazed donut, and my shoes would be full of hardened mud. For the moment, however, I was cool and comfortable lying there. I only prayed that Felix had found the other missing puppy.

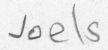

5

Let Sleeping Dogs Lie

"Not a word to Sam," I told Felix. "We'll just pretend like the puppies have been here all along." I bent over the wall of the Puppy Corral and set the last, moist puppy in among its brothers and sisters.

"I'm with you," Felix said. "Let's just let sleeping dogs lie."

Just as I straightened up, the glass door on the back of Sam's house slid open. Sam stood in the doorway looking out at us. I put on my most innocent smile.

"I thought you guys would have been long gone by now," Sam said. She came out into the yard and closed the door behind her. She walked around the Puppy Corral studying it. "It looks great," she said. "It's just what I needed. I owe you guys big time."

Sam finally looked at me. She stared at my torn, grease-streaked T-shirt. She looked down at my muddy, grass-stained, paint-streaked jeans. She reached up and pulled a large twig from my matted, muddy hair. She looked over at Felix. He didn't look much better.

"Wow," she said. "I thought you said the Puppy Corral was a piece of cake to assemble. You guys look like you barely survived some kind of explosion."

I glanced at Felix. "We had some unexpected complications," I said. Boy, was that the truth!

Sam stepped into the corral. "How are my babies?" she said. The puppies went wild with excitement. Nine puppies jumped and pounced and rolled. Nine tails wagged wildly. Sam kneeled down and played with them.

I looked over at Felix and smiled. We'd gotten away with it. We'd dodged a bullet. We'd pulled a fast one.

Sam stood up suddenly. "Hey," she said, "what's the deal here? What are you guys trying to pull?"

My stomach dropped. Felix's mouth fell open. He looked at me in a panic.

"What's the matter?" I asked, trying to keep the innocent smile on my face. "You've got a nice new Puppy Corral. All nine puppies are safe and sound. What's the problem?"

She looked at me skeptically. I felt my smile slip. "*That's* the problem," Sam said. "I've got *nine* puppies safe and sound."

"So?"

"I sold one of the puppies this morning," she said. "One of Aunt Kathy's neighbors drove out here before breakfast and picked one out. There were only *eight* puppies here when I left."

I just stood there blinking. "Eight puppies?" I said. Where had we gone wrong?

Sam looked down at the puppies swarming at her feet. She bent and picked one up. "This one's not mine," she said. "It's not even a golden retriever. I think it's an Irish setter."

I looked at the puppy in her hands. It did look a little different, now that she mentioned it. It was a darker cinnamon color, and it was a little bit bigger than the other pups.

I ransacked my mind for a plausible explanation. Felix was too fast for me. "We *stole* a puppy?" he blurted out to no one in particular. "We hijacked somebody's dog?"

Sam looked at him. I waved frantically for him to shut up, but it was no use.

"Now we're in trouble," Felix yelled at me. "Letting Sam's puppies go was one thing, but *stealing* a dog is probably a felony."

"What is he talking about?" Sam asked through clenched teeth.

"It's the heat," I said. "I think he's lost his mind."

"We're *dog nappers*," Felix went on in a panic. "The police are probably looking for us right now. This is all your fault, Willie."

"Relax," I told Felix. "It was an honest mistake. We'll just take the puppy back. Everything will be fine."

"Take it back?" Felix sputtered. "Take it back where? How do we know where that stupid puppy came from? We were finding puppies all over the place."

"What are you guys talking about?" Sam asked. Her voice had raised slightly.

"We'll just go door to door until we find the right house," I said, trying to calm Felix down.

"We covered a hundred square miles today," Felix exaggerated. "Do you know how many doors that is?"

"What's going on here?"

I sighed. There was only one thing to do. We had a lot of ground to cover, and we could use Sam's help to find where the extra puppy belonged. I told her the whole story. I tried to emphasize how kind I'd been to make her the Puppy Corral, and how easy it was to leave a gate open when you were carrying an armful of plastic pipes. I got all the way up to where Sam had come out through the glass door.

"That's where you came in," I told her. "You know the rest."

Sam didn't seem at all surprised by the story, but then she's known me a long time.

Sam knocked on all the doors and did the talking. She told us to stay well behind her when she knocked. She said that anyone who looked through their peephole to see my muddy hair and stained clothes wouldn't dare open the door. It was after 4:00 when we finally located the owner of the Irish setter pup.

"My numskull friends thought it was my golden retriever puppy," she explained to the woman, handing her the red pup. "Those two couldn't tell the difference between a poodle and a pit bull. We're terribly sorry."

The woman stared skeptically at Felix and me a few seconds. We must have looked a fright. I tried to smooth down my muddy hair with my fingers. The woman just pushed the door closed. We heard her lock several locks. Who could blame her?

I was ready to go home and take a cool shower, but I suddenly remembered something else I'd accidentally stolen: Mrs. Lawton's house number.

"Want to come over and play with the puppies?" Sam asked. "I'll make some more iced tea."

"No. You and Felix go on without me," I told her. "I've got to go over to Mrs. Lawton's house. I'll catch you guys tomorrow."

As soon as I knocked on Mrs. Lawton's door I reached in my pocket for the brass number. It was gone. Then it hit me. Before I'd left the house that morning I'd changed into jeans. The number was still in my shorts.

I stood there a minute wondering what I should do. I had the impulse to run away. After all, when Mrs. Lawton answered the door and saw me covered with mud and paint, what would I say? Trick or treat?

There was a shuffling noise on the other side of the door. It was too late to make a run for it. The door creaked open.

"Willie Plummet!" Mrs. Lawton said. Her mouth fell open. "Oh my! What happened to you? Were you in some kind of accident? Come right inside."

I had to hand it to the old lady: yesterday she found me passed out on her porch and today she found me covered with mud, yet she didn't bat an eyelash. I didn't have to say a word. I didn't have to explain why I was there. I just followed her into the house.

The fans were running in the hallway, and the house was a lot cooler. Mrs. Lawton led me to a small bathroom. In the mirror over the sink I finally saw what I looked like: I was in much worse shape than Felix. I washed my face and tried to rinse the mud from my hair in the sink. Once I'd gotten the dirt off my face and arms, I found some cuts and scratches I didn't even know I had. Mrs. Lawton gave me some cotton balls and hydrogen peroxide.

By the time we were done, her sink was full of mud and grease, and two of her white towels were black with grime, but she didn't seem to mind. I had a bump on my head from where I'd banged it under the minivan, so Mrs. Lawton sat me down in the parlor and fetched me some ice in a plastic bag to take the swelling down. When I was completely taken care of, Mrs. Lawton brought us some lemonade and sat down in the parlor with me. After the day I'd had, it was the best lemonade I'd ever tasted.

"You seem to lead a very active life," Mrs. Lawton said, sitting across from me in a big leather armchair. "You remind me of myself when I was a bit younger."

At that moment, something very unexpected began to happen: I began to have fun. Mrs. Lawton and I started swapping stories about all the knuckle-headed things we'd done. I told her about when I got stuck writing an advice column in the school paper and managed to knock our baseball team out of the playoffs, and she told me about the time she accidentally pushed John Wayne into a swimming pool with all his clothes on. I told her about the practical jokes I played on my neighbor, Phoebe, and she told me the pranks she played on her husband Wendell. I was amazed we had so much in common. The next thing I knew, the clock on the mantle chimed 7:00, and I was late for dinner!

"Do come back for another visit, Willie," Mrs. Lawton said from the doorway as I jogged down her porch steps. "I had an awful lot of fun hearing your stories."

"I have to come back," I told her. "I have to give you your 2." She looked puzzled, so I pointed up at the brass numbers over her door. Mrs. Lawton stepped outside and looked up at them.

"Why you've given me a new house number, Willie," Mrs. Lawton said. "How very thoughtful. Now perhaps I'll get more mail."

I just started laughing. And I laughed most of the walk home.

The next morning was a bit cooler, so I headed over to Sam's house to see how the Puppy Corral was working out. I made sure I had Mrs. Lawton's house number in my pocket before I left home.

When I got to Sam's house, there was a fancy black Lexus parked outside. It wasn't something I saw very often in our neighborhood, so I walked around it a couple of times, looking at the glossy black paint and gleaming chrome. Whoever owned it took good care of it.

I went up to Sam's front door and knocked. Mrs. Stewart took me out to the backyard. A woman and a couple of young kids—a boy and a girl—were looking the six remaining puppies over. The three of them were very well dressed. The girl had curly, well-brushed blonde hair. They had obviously arrived in the Lexus.

"I've been getting calls all morning," Sam told me, "from Pepperville and Cedarville and all over. That ad worked wonders. I've already sold Shawna and Sky."

"So you're raking in the bucks, huh?"

"Yeah," she said, "but it's kind of sad. I hate to see them go. I really love the little guys."

"Who are *these* guys?" I asked, gesturing over at the family. The blonde girl pointed at a puppy.

"They're from up in Cedar Heights," she told me. "The little girl wants a puppy for her birthday." Sam glanced over at them and then stepped closer to me. "She seems like a spoiled brat," Sam whispered. I looked over at the three of them.

"Not *that* one," the boy whined. "Pick a good one."

"That is a good one, stupid" the girl snapped. "It's gonna be *my* puppy. So *I* get to pick it."

"Just because you're ugly doesn't mean you have to pick an ugly dog," the boy said.

I looked at the mom. She didn't do anything. She didn't even seem to notice. If it had been my mom, those kids would have been in big trouble.

"Whatever dog I get, I'm going to train him to bite you," the girl said.

"If that thing bites me, it's going down the laundry chute," the boy told her.

The glass door behind Sam's house opened. A young boy came through, pulling a man by the hand. The man laughed as the boy towed him over to the puppy corral. The boy stood looking down at the puppies. The man kneeled behind him and looked over his shoulder. One of the puppies came over to the boy and climbed up on the fence with his front paws. The boy's face lit up, and he gently scratched the puppy behind the ears.

The mom in the other family picked up one of the other pups and came over to Sam.

"We'd like to buy this one," the woman told Sam curtly.

"*I* don't want that one," the boy said. "Megan's the only one who wants it."

The little girl reached up and began tugging at the puppy's tail. "Let *me* have it, Mom," the girl said. "It's *my* puppy."

The mother ignored her daughter. "I'm assuming it has papers," the woman said to Sam.

I watched Sam's face. She looked at the little, helpless puppy in this woman's arms. She looked down at the little girl pulling the puppy's tail. Sam's face seemed to harden. "I'm sorry," Sam said decisively. "These puppies aren't for sale."

The woman bristled. "Nonsense," she said. "I'll give you five hundred dollars for this dog." The boy and the girl seemed stunned into silence. They looked up at Sam with their mouths slightly open.

"Sorry," Sam said firmly. "It's not for sale."

The woman abruptly held the puppy out to Sam. Sam took it. "Come along, you two," the woman said. She stormed to the glass door and pulled it open. The little girl kept looking over her shoulder at Sam as she walked to the door. "Come *along*," the woman snarled at her.

Once the glass door slammed shut, Sam went over to the little boy with his father. The boy was still gently stroking the pup who had come to him.

"Can I help you?" Sam asked.

"Oh, we were just looking," the man said. "We can't really afford one. We'll probably end up going to the pound."

Sam looked back at the boy. He was very gentle and careful with the puppy. "Can't afford it?" Sam said. "Why that's the runt of the litter. We're giving that one away free. I'd appreciate it if you'd take it off our hands."

I looked at Sam. She winked at me. I smiled.

"Really?" the man said. He looked at his son and grinned. "Why, we'd love to take it off your hands."

Sam took the man and his son inside to fill out some papers, and I climbed in the Puppy Corral and played with the last five puppies. Fifteen minutes later, Sam came back out with a couple of glasses of iced tea. She handed one to me, and I took a sip.

"You pass up 500 dollars and then turn around and give one away free," I said. "You're not much of a businesswoman."

"No, I'm not," she admitted. "But I really care about those pups, and some things are more important than money."

6

My Dogs Are Killing Me

When I left Sam's house, I headed over to Mrs. Lawton's. I was a few houses away from her place when I saw her front door open. She came down the front steps to the sidewalk.

"Mrs. Lawton," I called. "I was just coming to see you."

"Why, how kind of you, Willie," she said smiling. "I was just on my way to the park, but I'd much rather visit with you."

"Why don't we do both?" I suggested. "There's a nice breeze today. I can walk to the park with you."

"Nonsense," she said. "There's no one at the park but old people. They'll bore you to death. All they talk about is arthritis and bunions, and there's nothing there for a young man like you to do."

"No," I told her. "I'll be fine. It'll be fun just to talk to you. If I get bored, I'll throw rocks in the pond."

Mrs. Lawton looked at me a moment. "I wonder if I can still skip a stone," she said. We started walking toward the park. "I once got 11 bounces on Lake Arrowhead, but that was when I was a young girl of 61."

I laughed.

When we got to the park, there were quite a few old people already there. It was warm but comfortable, especially under the shade of the sycamore trees. We walked down toward the duck pond. We passed the gazebo with its peeling paint and the weedy flower beds. I looked at all the dead grass. It was kind of sad to think that Mrs. Lawton and her friends didn't have a prettier place to hang out.

Mrs. Lawton chose a seat on a long bench beside a couple of old women. I sat down next to her on the end of the bench.

"Willie," Mrs. Lawton said. "I'd like you to meet Mildred and Eunice." She turned to the old women. "Girls," she said. "I'd like you to meet Willie Plummet, the famous inventor."

We sat in silence for a few moments. I watched the ducks swim.

"This hot weather really brings out my bronchitis," Mildred said. "Then the cold weather is terrible for my rheumatism."

There were a few more seconds of silence.

"My dogs are killing me," Eunice said suddenly. "They get so swollen in the summer I can barely get my shoes on."

Mildred nodded sympathetically.

Mrs. Lawton looked over at me and winked. "I've been having trouble with my sinuses," she said. "I think it's all this dry air."

The other two old women murmured condolences. Mrs. Lawton looked over at me and raised her eyebrows. I guessed it was my turn.

"I banged my head under a minivan yesterday," I volunteered. "But we put some ice on it, and it's feeling much better."

The two old women nodded approvingly at me. I guess I'd been accepted to the ranks: I was an honorary senior citizen. When I looked at Mrs. Lawton, her eyes were glittering with suppressed laughter. She winked at me again.

We probably sat there more than an hour chatting with Mildred and Eunice. Mrs. Lawton had me repeat some of my stories to the old women, and they laughed and shook their heads. I told them about losing Sam's pups and accidentally stealing an Irish setter. We had a great time. Finally, Mrs. Lawton said we had to be getting along. When we'd said our goodbyes, I started up the path we'd come down.

"Aren't you forgetting something?" Mrs. Lawton said.

I turned around. I had no idea what she was talking about.

"I thought we were going to skip some stones," Mrs. Lawton said, pretending to pout.

"Stones," I said. "Yeah, I forgot."

"Find me a good flat one," she said. "I'll bet I can still do it." She walked down to the steep bank of the pond. I thought about how I'd slipped and fallen in yesterday, and it worried me that she was so close to the water's edge. I hunted up a handful of stones and handed her the flattest one I could find.

Mrs. Lawton curled an old, thin finger around the stone and brought her arm back. I was afraid she was going to follow the stone into the water, so I asked her to take a couple of steps away from the water's edge.

"You're trying to make it harder for an old woman?" she asked me.

"I just don't want you to fall in," I told her truthfully. "Believe me, it can happen."

Mrs. Lawton looked at me like it had been a long time since anyone had worried about her. It was clear that she was touched. It made me a little uncomfortable. I thought maybe she'd start crying or something. Instead, she brought her arm back again and flung that stone out over the water. It didn't go very far, and it didn't spin very well, but it bounced once on the surface before it disappeared under the water.

Mrs. Lawton turned to me smiling. "Well what do you think of that, Willie Plummet?"

I smiled. "You throw like a girl."

She grinned. "Why that's the nicest thing anyone's said to me all summer," she said.

I walked Mrs. Lawton back to her house, and then I went home. As soon as I got up to my bedroom, I remembered the brass 2 in the pocket of my shorts. I'd have to go see Mrs. Lawton again tomorrow. I just smiled.

In fact I went to Mrs. Lawton's house a lot in the weeks before summer camp. I visited her nearly every afternoon after I'd done stuff with Sam and Felix or helped out at the hobby shop. Mrs. Lawton seemed to enjoy having me around, and to be honest, I loved being with her too. She laughed at all my dumb jokes, and she kept encouraging me to tell her stories.

I told her about when I used to deliver packages by dogsled and about the time I ran for class president. I told about how Sam, Felix, and I set off the Great Glenfield UFO Scare and about how I once tried to form my own rock band. She hung on my every word, and sometimes she laughed so hard I had to stop talking so she could catch her breath.

She told me funny stories about the famous people she'd met and about all the exotic places she'd visited. She spoke softly and sometimes chuckled to herself. Each story she told seemed to revolve around her dead husband, Wendell, so even though they were funny, they were a little sad.

Sometimes we'd just sit in the parlor and sip lemonade while the clock on the mantle ticked softly. It wasn't awkward or uncomfortable; it was peaceful. It was pleasant to just sit there with her.

I never did give her the brass number from above her door. I carried it in my pocket, but I'd always leave it there. It was kind of a running joke with us. I'd keep it so I'd have an excuse to come see her the next day.

"Do you ever take pictures anymore?" I asked her on the Thursday before I left for summer camp. I was looking through an old *Life* magazine that had some of her photographs in it.

"Oh, I haven't taken a portrait since my Wendell died," she said.

"But you have all that talent," I said. "I don't know anyone who can take photos like these. It seems like such a waste."

"It's nothing to have talent," Mrs. Lawton said. "It just means you can do something well. What you need is the desire to do something with your talent."

"I don't understand."

"Well, when my Wendell died, I didn't feel much like using my talent again. It was something we used to do together, seeing the world, meeting famous people. All that changed when Wendell died. It was like I'd lost my best friend."

"It's a shame," I said, turning a page in the magazine. "I'm sure there're lots of people who would still
love to have their picture taken by you."

"Well, there's only one famous person I'd be will-
ing to come out of retirement for," she said with a
faint smile. "If he asked me, I'd be happy to take his
portrait. I think you can guess who he is."

I tried to. I tried to think of the actor or musician
or artist she might be talking about. I had no idea.
"Who?" I asked.

"The famous inventor, Willie Plummet," she said.

I grinned. "Really?" I said. "You'd take my picture? Can we do it now? Should we do it outside?"

Mrs. Lawton shook her head. "We'll do it out on
the front porch," she said. "But now is the wrong
time. The best outdoor photos are taken early in the
morning or late in the afternoon. That's when the
lighting is best. Why don't you come back around
6:00? I'll have everything ready."

I had some time to kill, so I went over to Sam's
house. She'd sold all the puppies, but I'd never both-
ered to dismantle the Puppy Corral. Sam said she'd
help me take it apart. She said we could load the
pieces in the back of her mom's station wagon, and
they'd bring them over to my house when they picked
me up for church camp on Friday afternoon.

Felix was there when I arrived. We all sat in the
grass around the Puppy Corral.

"I hate to take this thing apart," Sam said, struggling to twist apart one of the plastic joints. "I really miss having the puppies around. They were a handful, but I loved them."

"You only had them a few days," Felix pointed out.

"Sometimes a few days is enough to really love something," Sam told him. She gritted her teeth and twisted the pipe with all her strength.

"What*ever*," Felix said. He wasn't the sentimental sort.

"I can't budge this," Sam said. "See if you can get it off, Willie."

I slid over to where Sam was sitting. I tried to twist the pipe out of its socket, but it was firmly stuck in place. "A pair of pliers would help," I told Sam.

"Gotcha," Sam said. "Be right back." She jumped up and disappeared into the house through the sliding glass door. Felix and I were alone.

"Did she tell you?" Felix whispered when Sam was safely out of hearing.

"Did who tell me what?"

"Sam," Felix said from the opposite side of the Puppy Corral. "Did Sam tell you that she *lost* 38 dollars in this whole puppy venture? Some businesswoman! I'm glad I wasn't an investor!" Felix seemed strangely full of glee.

"She knew what she was doing," I told Felix. "She did a good job."

"A good job?" Felix sputtered. "She could have made over a thousand dollars, and instead she lost 38 bucks. How is that a good job?"

I thought of Sam and her puppies. I thought of Mrs. Lawton and her house full of valuable collectibles. "Some people find value in things beyond how much money they're worth," I told Felix. "There are more important things than money."

Felix glared over at me. "There you go again," he said.

"Where am I going again?"

"You're climbing up on your high horse and looking down on the rest of us," Felix said. "Just because I want to make some money to pay for church camp, doesn't mean you're better than me."

"I didn't say that," I protested, but Felix slid around so his back was turned to me. He pretended he was pulling up one of the tent stakes with his thumb.

"Felix," I said. He ignored me the rest of the afternoon.

When I climbed the porch steps a little before 6:00, Mrs. Lawton was waiting for me on the porch swing. She had set up a large fabric reflector on one side of the swing. I could see what she meant about the afternoon light; the whole porch glowed golden and warm. When Mrs. Lawton smiled at me her face looked warm and full of life. The sunlight glimmered in her eyes. She was an old woman, but she was pretty just the same. In that light, I could imagine the younger face I'd seen in some of the old photographs in her house.

"You sit right here, and we'll shoot a whole roll," she told me. "We'll try some different things. We'll get a good shot. I just know we will."

I sat down on the porch swing, and Mrs. Lawton went over behind the camera on the tripod. She looked through the lens and made a couple of adjustments, and then straightened up and looked at me.

"Turn your head a little that way," she told me. "Now sit back a little and tilt your head up a little."

I tried to do as she told me, even though I sometimes ended up in uncomfortable positions. I'd always felt a little self-conscious posing for photographs, but Mrs. Lawton kept talking and telling me stories as we took the photos, and that relaxed me a bit. I even got so I could ignore the cars passing by that slowed down to see what we were doing. Every time Mrs. Lawton said something that made me laugh, I'd hear the shutter click, and she'd wind the film ahead. She was very good at what she did.

"Six more, and we'll have shot the whole roll," she told me looking down at the camera. "Are there any poses you'd like to try?"

"How about a few of us both together?"

Mrs. Lawton smiled softly. "Why, I'd love to have my photo taken with the famous Willie Plummet," she said. "You'll have to sign it, and I'll add it to all the others."

She looked through the lens again and adjusted her tripod. She set the timer on the camera and came over to sit beside me. I leaned in close to her, and the shutter clicked.

When we'd finished off the roll, Mrs. Lawton took the camera off the tripod and showed me how to wind the film back into its canister, and then she handed me the camera.

I looked at her. "Do you want me to take the film out?"

"You can do what you want," she said. "It's your camera."

"What?"

"I want you to have it, Willie," she told me. "It's a good camera, and I'm not going to be using it. I'd like you to have it."

I was stunned. "I can't accept this," I said. "It must be worth hundreds of dollars. I know you have a son. Maybe he'd want it."

"Oh, believe me," she said, "he'll be getting everything I own. But he doesn't care about any of it. He'll just sell everything for as much cash as he can get, and that will be the end of it."

"That couldn't be true," I told her. "I'm sure he cares about all your stuff."

Mrs. Lawton looked out at the street. The afternoon sun shone on her face and lit up her eyes. I thought I saw tears forming. "I love my son," she told me. "But I wish he was a lot more like you, Willie." She dabbed at her eyes with the sleeve of her blouse. When she turned to look at me she was smiling again. "Please take the camera, Willie. I want you to have it. It'll remind you of me when I'm gone."

I felt a lump in my throat. I didn't like to hear her talk that way, but I knew I'd have to take the camera. It would mean a lot to both of us.

The first thing in the morning, I took the canister of film to Shaw's Photo and Framing and dropped it off to be developed. I looked at the framed letters and signed photographs high on the wall behind the counter. They were nice, but they were nothing compared to the stuff in Mrs. Lawton's house.

"You can pick it up Tuesday afternoon," Mr. Shaw told me, tearing the claim ticket off the envelope flap and handing it to me.

"No rush," I told him. "I'll be at camp until Friday. I'll probably come get it as soon as I get back."

"Have a good time," he told me.

I jumped on my bike and headed over to Mrs. Lawton's house.

"I just wanted to come and say good-bye before I headed off to camp," I told her, standing on her front porch. "And I finally remembered to bring you your house number." I took it out of my pocket and held it out to her.

"I'd rather you held on to it until after camp," she told me from the doorway. "That way you'll be sure to come visit when you get back."

I smiled. "Of course I'm going to come visit."

"And you'll tell me about any adventures you have at camp?"

"If I don't have any, I'll make some up," I said. I looked at her a long time. "I'm really going to miss you, Mrs. Lawton." It was the truth. Who'd ever have thought a guy like me would end up with a friend like her?

"And I'm going to miss you too, Willie."

"I'm taking your camera," I told her. "And I'll take lots of pictures of everything that happens."

"Why, that will be wonderful," she told me.

I stood there a moment, not sure what to do. Then I just stepped up to her and gave her a big hug. When I let go of her and stepped back, she was smiling, and her eyes were tearing up.

I smiled. "You cry like a girl," I told her.

Mrs. Lawton laughed and dabbed at her eyes with the sleeve of her blouse. "Why, Willie, you sure know how to give an old woman a compliment," she said.

7

A Dog's Life

When Mrs. Stewart pulled her station wagon up in front of my house, I was all ready to go. I'd stuffed my duffel bag with clothes, a toothbrush, a Bible, the camera, and a flashlight. Sam and Felix helped me unload the dismantled Puppy Corral and carry it to the garage. Then we put my sleeping bag and my duffel bag in the back, and we were on our way.

"This had better be good," Felix said as the car pulled away from the curb. "I had to pay for this camp myself."

By the time we got to Shepherd of the Hills Camp, it was late in the afternoon. We pulled up on the gravel in front of the camp office. When we opened the doors of Mrs. Stewart's station wagon, it was suddenly cold. I got out and stretched. We'd been on the road a long time.

"Feel that?" I said, rubbing the goose bumps from my arms. "Isn't it wonderful to be cold?"

"I'd forgotten what it was like," Sam said.

Mr. Trumble, the camp leader, was with all the other kids at the fire ring for orientation. A woman in the office told us which cabins we were in. Sam headed over to the girls' cabins with her mom. Felix and I carried our stuff to the boys' side of the camp. We were assigned to a new cabin that had just been built this summer. When we went through the front doors, we found ourselves in a big room with a fireplace and a bunch of chairs and benches. Everything still smelled of lumber and sawdust.

"This must be the lobby," Felix said.

On the back wall was another door. I went over and pushed the door open. Behind it was the bunk room. Most of the bunks had sleeping bags unrolled on them, and suitcases or duffel bags. One bunk in the corner was completely empty.

"How about we take that one?" I said.

"Sure," Felix said. He lugged his stuff across to the empty bunk, and I followed him.

"How do we decide who gets to be on top?" I asked.

Felix snorted and threw his sleeping bag on the top bunk. "*I* do, of course," he said.

"Why you?"

Felix threw his duffel bag up beside his sleeping bag. "I had to pay my own way to this camp," he said. "I'd better get the top bunk." He climbed up and started unrolling his sleeping bag.

"You know," I said. "I didn't get to come here free. My mom and dad had to pay my way."

"Well, when they show up, they can sleep up here with me," Felix told me.

I sighed and plopped my stuff down on the bottom bunk. "You think you're funny," I told Felix. "But you're not." I unzipped my duffel bag, grabbed a sweatshirt and pulled it over my head.

Just then there was a clanging noise from outside in the dark.

"That must be dinner," I said.

"Good," Felix said, leaping down from his bunk. "I'm starving. It must be the mountain air. I don't think I've ever been so hungry."

We found our way to the dining hall and got in line. Sam joined us. No one seemed to mind.

"Are you guys as hungry as I am?" Sam asked, rubbing her hands together.

"You bet," Felix said. "This better be good. After all—"

"*You paid your own way,*" Sam finished the sentence for him. "We know. We know."

The line moved ahead, and we passed through the dining hall door.

"You'll be happy to hear that they've got a brand new chef this week," Sam said. "He must be good; he used to have his own restaurant."

"Restaurant food at a camp," Felix said. "I like the sound of that."

"They must have hired the guy once they heard you paid your own way." I said to Felix. "I'm surprised they haven't found you a butler yet."

Felix grabbed a tray and stepped up to the serving line. Sam and I followed him. A huge man stood there behind the counters. He was wearing one of those tall chef's hats. "Vhat would you like, little boy?" he asked Felix with a thick foreign accent.

I looked up at the chef. He was kind of grim looking.

"What *is* this stuff?" Felix whispered over to me.

I looked down at the trays of gray and reddish foods. No hot dogs, no French fries, no beans. It didn't look like any camp food I'd ever seen. There wasn't a single thing behind the glass I recognized.

"This is the borscht," the man said. "Here is the goulash. Over here vee have the cabbage rolls. And this is the smoked tongue with paprika gravy."

Smoked tongue? Felix glanced over at me and then looked back down at the food. He suddenly didn't look as hungry as he had a moment ago. He rubbed the back of his neck with his hand.

"I'll have some of the reddish stuff and some of that green stuff," Felix said, pointing at some of the trays that *weren't* smoked tongue.

Sam was next. "I couldn't help but notice your accent," she said politely. "Where do you come from?"

The tall man smiled happily. He gathered himself up even taller and put a hand to his chest. "I am Mr.

Kocsis," he said proudly. "I am from Budapest. I owned restaurant there. Now I come to America."

Back at the table Felix lifted a forkful of red stuff to his nose and sniffed at it. By the look on his face, it didn't smell any better than it sounded.

"He's from Hungary," Sam said. "It's a different culture. They eat different foods. *They'd* probably think *our* food was weird."

Felix nibbled at the stuff on his fork and made a face. "No wonder they call the place Hungry," he said.

"Not *Hungry*," Sam told him. "Hung*ary*."

"Whatever," Felix said. "I was looking forward to some good camp food. You know—hamburgers and potato chips."

"I'm sure this is good food," Sam said. "The man owned his own restaurant. He must be a good cook. If we were Hungarian-Americans, we'd probably love this stuff."

"Well I'm a hungry American, and I want American food," Felix said. He set his fork down on his tray and sighed.

"Don't be so rude and closed-minded," Sam scolded him. "At least give it a try." Sam stabbed a piece of cabbage roll with her fork and popped it into her mouth. She chewed quickly at first, but then she slowed down. She squeezed her eyes tight shut and swallowed, then took a quick gulp from her glass of milk.

I had to hand it to Sam. She gave it her best. But even *she* wasn't able to finish half of the food on her plate. By now, the usual cafeteria noise had died down. There was no clattering of plates or clinking of silverware. No one spoke. An odd silence filled the room.

I glanced around at the other tables. Plates were still piled high with food. No one was eating. Everyone looked hungry and depressed.

Mr. Trumble tried to lead us in singing at the campfire meeting, but it never really got off the ground. When he dismissed us, we all just went back to our cabins.

Lying there in my lower bunk in the dark, I couldn't sleep. I was so hungry, my stomach kept growling. I don't think anyone else in the cabin could sleep either. I could hear the other kids moving around on their bunks in the dark. No one was snoring. I knew we were all feeling the same way.

"Ever had one of those corn dogs with the cheese already inside it?" someone said.

"Yeah!" another voice said. "I *love* those."

I felt Felix stir in the bunk above me.

"They're really good if you dip them in chili each time you take a bite," a third voice chimed in.

"Chili cheese fries!" the first voice said again. "Now *that's* food! I love the first one, when the cheese is all stringy and steaming."

I felt Felix roll over again.

"It's kind of like the first slice of pizza," a voice said across the room. "You know how the cheese is still hot and stringy and when you pull—"

"*Shut up!*" Felix screamed suddenly in the dark. "*Nobody say another word!*" In the sudden quiet, I noticed that even the crickets outside had been stunned into silence. "I paid good money to come up here, and I am *not* a happy camper!" Felix growled. "I am *starving*, and I will personally strangle the next person who says anything about food. Now everyone *turn over* and *go to sleep*."

There were a few seconds of silence.

"*Turnovers*," someone said in the darkness. "I love the apple ones with that runny icing on top." There was lots of muffled laughter after that, but it was the last thing anyone said until morning.

The next morning in the dining hall, we had some kind of turnip stuffed with eggs and goat cheese for breakfast. I was so hungry, I managed to choke down a few bites, but that was all I could manage. I looked around at all the starving kids who had crowded the hall, hoping for something good to eat after last night's dinner. They looked depressed. I looked over at Felix. He was more depressed than any of them.

"Have I mentioned that I had to pay my own way to camp this year?" he said, studying the goat cheese that dangled from his fork.

"Yes, I believe you have mentioned it," Sam said coldly. "Have I mentioned that you're the most annoying person I've ever met?" It wasn't often that Sam got angry at anyone, but she wasn't in a very good mood that morning. Everyone's temper seemed a bit frayed, and I was no exception. Every person I saw that morning was getting on my nerves. I couldn't wait to get away on my own. It's funny how being hungry can change a person's whole outlook on life.

"I'm sorry," Felix said, pushing his plate away. "It's just ticking me off. I wish I'd stayed at home. Home's free—and at least I get some decent food to eat."

Sam and I didn't say anything. I suppose she was wishing she'd stayed home too, she just didn't say it out loud. I sat with my elbows on the table and my chin in my hands. I was looking at a plate full of turnip, but I was thinking about pancakes and bacon and fried eggs and sausages.

After a while Sam sighed. "I'd give 20 dollars for a decent meal," she said.

"Me too," I said.

"It's unanimous," Felix moaned.

After breakfast, we did some group activities, then were given some free time. None of us were in the mood for company. I took a long walk around the lake with the camera Mrs. Lawton had given me. I took some shots of the pines reflected in the water. I skipped lunch—there didn't seem to be any point in getting in line at the dining hall. I stayed out at the lake until the afternoon so I could get the good lighting Mrs. Lawton told me about. I thought about her sitting in her big old house right now. I wished I was there with her. I couldn't think of anyone else I wanted to hang around with right now.

I got back to the cabin before dinner. Usually at camp all the kids would be busy with crafts or activities in the late afternoon, or they'd be out on the lake in canoes or fishing from the dock. But everyone in our cabin seemed to be hanging out in the front room lounging on the chairs and benches, no doubt dreaming about food.

Felix was there too. A fire was roaring in the fireplace, but he was wearing his hooded sweatshirt. He seemed in an awfully good mood for someone who was starving.

"I missed lunch today," I said to Felix. "Was there anything good to eat?" All the kids hanging around the front room groaned irritably at my question.

"They had some kind of eggplant casserole," Felix whispered. "Isn't it wonderful?"

"*Wonderful*?" I said. "Eggplant?"

Felix motioned for me to follow him. He led me into the bunk room and closed the door. He glanced around to make sure we were alone.

"Guess what *I* did today?" he asked. He was obviously excited.

"You personally told every camper that you paid your way to camp this year?" I guessed.

"No," he whispered. He glanced around himself again. "I talked a couple of counselors into going into town for me."

"*So*?" I said. "What's the big deal?"

"Keep your voice down," he begged.

"What*ever*," I said. "What's the big secret?"

"Our Hungarian chef no longer has a monopoly in this camp," Felix whispered. "I'm the new competition."

"I don't get it. What are you talking about?"

"Remember that list of things to bring to camp?" Felix asked. "The one they handed out in Sunday school?"

"Yeah."

"How much money did it say to bring?"

"You *know* what it said," I told him. "It recommended that we all bring 20 dollars in spending money even though there's nothing up here to spend it on."

"*Exactly*," Felix said. "There's more than 100 kids up here. At 20 dollars each, that's more than *2,000 dollars!* And there's nothing to spend it on!"

"So?" I said. Sometimes Felix took a while to get to the point, and I was in no mood to be patient with him today.

"If you were back in Glenfield, what would you buy right now with your 20 bucks?"

I laughed. "Well, *duh*," I said. "I'd buy a decent meal."

"Exactly!" Felix could barely contain his excitement. He reached inside the pouch in his sweatshirt and pulled out a package of hot dogs.

The minute I saw the package my stomach growled. I could have torn the package open and eaten them raw. "Man!" I gasped. "When do we eat?"

"Not so fast, Willie." Felix stuffed the package back in his sweatshirt. "We're not going to eat up my investment."

"Investment?"

"These dogs cost me about 45 cents each—that's including the bun," Felix said. "That's not accounting for the big bottle of mustard or the box of wire coat hangers." He squinted up at the cabin ceiling, doing the math in his head. "If I sell them for two dollars apiece, that's a 300 percent profit margin."

"You're going to *sell* them?" I sputtered. "I've got a better idea. You, me, and Sam eat them all."

"Dude, you're not getting the picture," Felix said. "The counselors bought every hot dog in that general store for me. I've got more than 300 hot dogs hidden in my bunk. I've got 264 buns—and a few loaves of bread for when we run out of those."

I couldn't believe it. This was weird even for Felix. I pushed past him and went over to the corner where our bunks were. Felix's blanket barely covered a mound of hot dogs and buns that nearly touched the ceiling. I stared at it, speechless. It was a mountain of food—the most American kind of food there is. It nearly brought tears to my eyes.

"It's beautiful," I said.

"But it's *our* secret," Felix told me. "No one can know it's there."

"You call *that* a secret?" I said. "It looks like a Jiffy Pop container."

Felix eyed his bunk skeptically. "No one's going to notice, at least not until tonight."

"Where are you going to sleep?" I asked him.

He grinned. "On a big pile of money," he said. "I'm betting I sell every one of those hot dogs tonight. I have to give the couselors some of the profit, but I'm still practically a millionaire."

"Practically a psychopath is what *you* are," I told him shaking my head. "But if everyone at this camp is as hungry as I am, this might just work."

"Spread the word," Felix said. "Nine o'clock. At the fire. Two bucks a dog. Eight bucks for all you can eat."

He glanced up at his mountainous bunk one last time and headed for the door. He stopped in the doorway and turned back to look at me. "No free samples, Willie," he told me, wagging a finger in my direction. It was like he could read my mind.

Hot Dogs! Get 'Em While They're Hot!

When the campfire meeting ended that evening, no one left. The entire camp stayed huddled around the fire. Mr. Trumble hung around talking to some of the kids, surprised by how much camp unity had developed overnight. "This is good to see," I heard him say to one of the cabin counselors. "After last night's meeting, I was worried about this group." By 8:30, he excused himself and went back to his cabin. He said he had to be up at 5:00 in the morning.

When the counselors were sure Mr. Trumble wouldn't be back, they gave Felix the high sign. Felix stood up on a log with his back to the fire. "We will have two chefs working this evening," he announced. "So we will need you to divide into two lines."

Before he'd even finished his sentence, the loud shuffling and arguing began, and in less than a minute, there were two long lines winding back from the fire into the darkness where the light didn't reach.

Felix gave Sam and me straightened coat hangers to cook the hot dogs. He promised to pay us each two hot dogs to be his chefs. I wanted mine now, but one look at the kids and counselors in front of my line, and I knew I'd better feed them quick. I immediately skewered a hot dog and dangled it over the fire.

"When you get to the front of the line, let the chef know how you'd like your hot dog cooked," Felix said. "And please have your money ready."

Then it began. Sam and I both cooked two hot dogs at a time. It didn't really matter whether someone asked for rare or well done, we just stuck the franks in the fire a minute or so until they were brown and glistening, and then Felix slapped them in buns and handed them to the next person in line. One kid, who paid eight dollars for all he could eat, actually stood by me and ate nine hot dogs one after the other before he was satisfied.

An hour later, the front pouch of Felix's sweat shirt was stuffed with dollar bills, and the rest of us were stuffed with hot dogs. I even bought one myself; it had been so long since I'd eaten a decent meal, two free hot dogs just weren't enough.

"Tomorrow night. Same time, same place," Felix announced to the last few customers who lingered near the fire.

"Tomorrow night?" I whispered. "We only have a couple more packages."

"Don't worry," Felix grinned. "The counselors are sure to do this again. They'll get more. This is a sure thing." He patted his stuffed sweat shirt. "I must have close to 400 dollars in here."

"But you said you bought every hot dog in the store," I reminded him. "What if they don't have any tomorrow?"

"Relax, Willie," Felix assured me. "There's got to be more than one store in town."

With a full stomach, I slept like a log that night. In the morning, when the breakfast bell clanged, I just rolled over in my bunk and went back to sleep. I don't think a single kid in my cabin got out of bed for breakfast.

After our morning meeting, Felix, Sam, and I decided to do something together during our free time. We hadn't really spent much time in each other's company since we'd arrived in camp. It was Sam who suggested we do some crafts.

We headed across camp to the craft shop. This morning kids were running everywhere. Laughter and shouts filled the air. It was like a normal camp again. Canoes were out on the lake. Some kids were tossing horseshoes, and others were practicing archery. The whole camp was finally humming along, fueled by Felix's hot dogs.

Felix strutted between Sam and me like some kind of celebrity. Kids waved to him and told him they'd see him at the campfire tonight. Felix drank it all in.

"Free enterprise is a wonderful thing," Felix said, waving to a group of girls sitting on the front steps of their cabin. "You take these kids' money, and they love you for it."

I looked over at Sam. She just rolled her eyes. Felix could be pretty annoying.

"And you know how I managed to make a lot of money selling *my* dogs?" Felix asked Sam. "Because *I* didn't bother to give them all names." He started laughing at his own joke.

Sam didn't say anything, but I knew she was ticked. I thought of Sam's puppies. She'd grown to love them so much that finding them good homes was more important than making money. I wanted to stick up for her. "Sam could have made a lot of money," I told Felix. "But she was more concerned about the puppies. Money isn't the most important thing."

"Yeah," Felix said, "but it's pretty cool." I just shook my head.

The craft shop was a long cabin full of long benches. It smelled of glue and leather. We found an empty table, and the crafts counselor came over to see what we'd like to work on. There were three projects we could choose from: we could make a wallet, weave a wrist band, or assemble a picture frame. I chose the frame. I thought I'd make it for Mrs. Lawton. When I got home, I could go over to Shaw's Photo and Framing and pick up the photos she'd taken. I'd put one of them in the frame so she could hang it on the wall with all the photos of her famous friends.

"What do you want a stupid picture frame for?" Felix asked. "It's not like you've got a picture of some girlfriend that needs framing."

"Well, what are *you* making?" I asked him.

"*Duh*," he said. "I'm making a wallet. I'm going to need three or four of them to hold all my cash." He looked down at the rectangles of leather arranged on the craft table before him. "I wonder if they come in larger sizes," he said.

Felix was really annoying me. I glanced over at Sam. She was usually the one who kept us all in line. I was expecting her to scold Felix for being so greedy, but she was immersed in the wrist band she was weaving; either that or she was ignoring us. Her tongue poked out of the corner of her mouth. She didn't say a word.

"You know there's more to life than money," I said, since Sam hadn't.

"Yeah," Felix snorted. "There's picture frames."

I felt my jaw muscles tightening. "It's a *gift*," I informed him. "Some of us actually try to think of other people once in a while. I'm making this for Mrs. Lawton."

"Oh," Felix said. "I stand corrected. You *do* have a girlfriend whose photo you want to frame. She just happens to be a 110 years old."

I felt my face flush in anger. I clenched my fists.

"Lay off," Sam warned Felix, but it was too late. I was furious.

"What's with you?" I shouted. "You think the only thing worth working for is money? You think the only people worth spending time with are people your own age?"

Felix's eyes darted around the room. I could tell everyone in the craft shop had stopped working and was looking at us. I didn't care.

"She may be 80 years old," I said, "but right now Mrs. Lawton is a better friend than you are."

I stood up, scooped up the pieces of wood, and stormed off to an empty table. I sat there a few minutes with my back to Felix and Sam. My heart was pounding, and I tried to calm myself down. I looked down at the project I was working on.

I tried to clear my mind. The frame was easy to make, but I wanted to do the best job I could. It seemed really important right then, like this was more than a picture frame. It was like a symbol of something. I suppose it struck me right then that I really loved Mrs. Lawton. She *was* a good friend.

I forgot about Felix for a moment and thought of Mrs. Lawton. I thought of the camera she'd given me; I thought of all the stories she'd told me and all her encouraging words. I thought of her skipping a rock on the pond and taking my photo on the front porch. She made me happy, and I knew I did the same for her. This frame had to be special. I picked up two pieces of wood and the bottle of glue and set to work. I was so immersed in what I was doing, I didn't notice when Sam and Felix left the craft shop.

I took my time working. When I'd finally painted the frame with stain, it was nearly dinner time, and I was the only kid left in the craft shop. I looked down at the frame on the table before me. I'd done a good job, but there was nothing *special* about it. There was nothing about it that would let Mrs. Lawton know how much her friendship meant to me. It needed something more.

The crafts counselor helped me find some gold paint and a fine paint brush. I leaned in close, and in my neatest printing I painted some words from Proverbs along the bottom of the frame: "A friend loves at all times."

When I was done, I straightened up and looked at my work. Mrs. Lawton would love it.

When I got back to my cabin, Felix's bunk was again piled high with food and covered over with his sleeping bag. There was a note on my bunk.

> Willie—
>
> The counselors brought this back while you were still in the craft shop. I know you're mad at me, and I'm sorry I made fun of Mrs. Lawton. I hope you'll still help me tonight by being my chef. You can have all the hot dogs you want for free.
>
> —Felix

I was still pretty mad at Felix, but the words from Proverbs came back to me: "A friend loves at *all* times." I knew I shouldn't stay mad at him. Besides, I was hungry, and the thought of eating six or seven hot dogs made it a lot easier to be forgiving.

I sat next to Felix at the evening campfire meeting. He seemed genuinely glad to see me. Sam came and sat down on Felix's other side.

That night Mr. Trumble talked about contentment. I guess he'd heard some complaints from the campers about the food. He used 1 Timothy 6:6–11 as his text. He stood on the other side of the fire, holding an old, leather Bible. The fire lit his face up golden and red. Sometimes when he talked, he looked into the flames of the campfire instead of at us. He spoke loudly so we could hear him over the crackling of the big fire.

"'But godliness with contentment is great gain,'" Mr. Trumble read aloud from his Bible. "'For we brought nothing into the world, and we can take nothing out of it. But if we have food and clothing, we will be content with that.'"

At the mention of food, I immediately thought of the hot dogs we'd be cooking once this meeting was done. An empty stomach can be very distracting. After a few minutes, however, Mr. Trumble's words started to get through to me. He told us about how some people spent their whole lives trying to get more things, hoping they'd be happy. I thought of the family that offered Sam 500 dollars for one of her puppies. They would have played with the puppy for a week, and then gotten bored with it and started looking for something else.

Then I thought of Mrs. Lawton. She had all those valuable things in her house, but how much they were worth wasn't important to her. She only kept them because they reminded her of all the blessings God had given her—her good friends and her adventures with her husband Wendell. Yet even now, on her own, Mrs. Lawton was content and happy. She knew the most valuable thing she had was the love and forgiveness of Jesus, who had died and risen again for her and for all.

Mr. Trumble read some verses about how we shouldn't love money, and I could feel Felix squirm beside me. Felix wasn't such a bad guy. He was a good friend; he just sometimes got carried away.

"'But you, man of God,'" Mr. Trumble read near the end of his talk, "'flee from all this, and pursue righteousness, godliness, faith, love, endurance and gentleness.'"

All week I'd been telling Felix that there were more important things in life than money, but I'd never really thought of what those things were. Now here was a whole list of them. I knew which was most important: love.

After the campfire meeting was done, and Mr. Trumble had gone back to his cabin, Felix and I lugged our duffel bags full of hot dogs and buns out of our cabin and over to the fire. Sam lit our way with her flashlight.

"Wow," I said, puffing. "This thing is heavy. I didn't think you'd be able to find any more after you cleaned out that grocery store yesterday."

"The counselors found these at a health food store," Felix said. "They were even on special. I bought 600 of them."

"What kind of health food store sells *hot dogs*?" Sam laughed. "No one who goes in there would buy them."

Felix shrugged. "Maybe that's why they were on special," he said.

When we got to the fire, everyone was already in two lines. The ones near the front had their money out and waiting.

"If I stayed up here another week, I could make enough money to retire," Felix said.

I looked at the long line of kids in front of me, every one of them hungry and expectant. I tore open a package of hot dogs and skewered one on a coat hanger. I dangled it over the fire and ducked it in the flame a couple of times. Then something odd began to happen. Instead of turning a delicious glistening brown, it turned a bluish-purple color, like a bad bruise. A few seconds later it bubbled and twisted on the end of my coat hanger. I pulled the hot dog out of the fire and looked at it. It was a truly revolting sight: a purple, blistered knob of meat.

I blew on it to cool it down and then sniffed at it. It *smelled* like a hot dog, but it looked repulsive. I glanced over at Sam. She was studying the blue, twisted growth on the end of her own coat hanger.

"Felix?" I mumbled, trying not to draw the attention of the hungry crowd. "Felix? Maybe you should look at this."

Felix came around to my side of the fire. I showed him the hot dog.

"What *is* that?" he asked. A look of disgust came to his face.

"I was about to ask you the same thing."

Sam came around to our side of the fire. She showed us the hot dog on the end of her coat hanger. It looked worse than mine.

"Maybe it's a bad package of dogs," Felix whispered. He glanced over his shoulder at the long lines of campers waiting to be fed. "Try opening another pack."

Sam pulled another package of hot dogs from Felix's duffel bag and started to open it. She stopped suddenly. "Where did you say you got these hot dogs?" she asked.

"Some health food store," Felix said.

"Did you read the label?" Sam asked. She handed Felix the package of hot dogs.

"'Turkey and Tofu Fat-Free Wieners,'" Felix read. "What's that mean?"

"It means you can't roast them," Sam said. "There's no fat in them."

"Well, what do you do with them?" Felix said, his eyes growing wide.

"I don't know," Sam said. "I suppose you microwave them or something."

Felix looked down at the knob of steaming, purple meat on the end of Sam's coat-hanger. "What's it taste like?" Felix asked. "Maybe it just *looks* bad. Somebody take a bite."

None of us moved. I certainly wasn't going to taste that thing.

"Maybe if we put a lot of mustard on them no one will notice," Felix said.

I held the deformed hot dog up in front of his face. "It's kind of hard to miss, don't you think?" I said.

"What am I doing to do?" Felix said. "I'm bankrupt! I spent all my money on those stupid hot dogs. I'm ruined."

Dog and Pony Show

It was hard to sleep that night. All of us were hungry, and a lot of us were angry because we'd been expecting to eat our fill of hot dogs. I'm sure no one got less sleep than Felix. All through the night, I heard him tossing and turning up above me in a bunk full of fat-free turkey and tofu hot dogs.

When the sun started coming up, an idea began to form in my head.

"You awake?" I whispered up to Felix.

"Awake and broke," he moaned.

"I think I know a way we can make back some of your money," I told him. "Pack up those hot dogs."

In a few minutes we were lugging the duffel bags full of hot dogs over to the dining hall. The morning air was chilly. I could see Felix's breath in the air as he struggled with his duffel bag. We went around back to the kitchen door and knocked.

In a few seconds a very flustered Mr. Kocsis opened the door.

"Do you have a microwave oven we could use?" I asked politely.

Mr. Kocsis seemed too tired and distracted to notice no counselor was with us. He just stepped aside and let us come in. We found the microwave, and Mr. Kocsis went over to a wooden table where he was chopping cauliflower.

"Cauliflower for breakfast?" Felix said. "That's going to be a big hit."

I found a clean plate and put two hot dogs on it. I put them in the microwave and set it for one minute. While the hot dogs heated up, I watched Mr. Kocsis. As he chopped the cauliflower, he kept sighing. Something was obviously troubling him.

The bell on the microwave rang, and Felix opened the door. He slipped the steaming wieners into buns. He handed one to me. I studied the warm hot dog. It looked normal. I held it up under my nose and sniffed at it. It actually smelled pretty good.

"Let's hope they taste as good as they smell," I said. I raised the fat-free hot dog to my mouth. I was starving, but after seeing these things all twisted and blue last night, I only took a small bite. It wasn't bad. It didn't taste as good as a regular hot dog, but it was definitely the tastiest thing to come out of *this* kitchen all week.

I nodded my head. "I think this will work," I told Felix as he popped the last bit of his hot dog into his mouth. "Put another one in the microwave."

Just then Mr. Kocsis groaned. I stepped closer to him. "Is something the matter?" I asked him. He looked up from his cauliflower like he'd forgotten we were there.

He shook his head dejectedly. "You can't help me," he said.

"You never know," I said. " What seems to be the problem?"

"I don't understand you peoples," Mr. Kocsis said. "I've made every good recipe I know, but no one eats my food. How do you Americans stay alive without you eat? How will I keep my job without you eat?"

I looked down at the cauliflower and prepared to give him my sales pitch. "It's just that this food is all new to us," I said. "The kids would eat more if you sometimes gave them the kind of food they're used to."

Just then the microwave oven's bell rang. Felix opened the door and pulled out the hot dog. He brought it over to me in a bun.

"Here," I said, holding the hot dog out to Mr. Kocsis. "Try this. It's easy to fix, kids love them, and we can sell you enough to feed the entire camp."

Mr. Kocsis looked from me to Felix and back again. He took the hot dog from me and took a tiny bite. He made a face like he'd just tasted something terrible. "You *like* the taste of this?" he asked.

Felix looked at me and smiled.

"Yeah," I said. "We like it a lot."

Mr. Kocsis took another small bite and chewed it skeptically. "If I cook this, you kids will eat so I keep my job?" he asked.

"Absolutely," I said. "Kids love hot dogs."

Mr. Kocsis took another bite and nodded his head. "Where you have the hot dogs? We make the deal!"

As soon as we got out through the kitchen doors, Felix looked over at me like he might grab me and give me a big kiss. I backed away.

"You saved me from financial ruin," he said. "How will I ever repay you?"

I thought a moment. "You can repay me by selling the hot dogs to Mr. Kocsis for whatever money you came to camp with," I said.

"*What?*" Felix said. "What about my profit margin?"

"'But if we have food and clothing, we will be content with that,'" I quoted. "Besides, you'll be helping Mr. Kocsis keep his job."

Felix looked down at the ground as we walked. It was clear he didn't like the idea of giving up his profit, but he also he knew he was better off now than when he went to bed last night. "Okay," he said. "I brought 100 dollars with me, and that's what I'll go home with. Are you satisfied now?"

I grinned. "Looks like you just graduated the Samantha Stewart School of Business," I said.

"Huh?"

"You sold all your dogs and *still* didn't make a profit," I told him.

Felix looked at me and grinned. "You think you're funny," he told me, "but you're not."

We had a good time that day. Felix, Sam, and I went out on a canoe, and I got a lot of good pictures. By the time lunch rolled around, the rumor had swept through the camp that Mr. Kocsis was actually preparing hot dogs for lunch. After last night's disappointment at the campfire, everyone was thrilled.

Felix insisted that we go over to the dining hall 15 minutes before lunch to make sure we were first in line.

"I am so hungry, I'm going to eat my weight in turkey and tofu hot dogs," Felix said.

"I'm right with you," Sam said. "This is going to be great."

After a few mintues, Mr. Kocsis pulled the dining hall doors open. He looked expectant and happy.

"Ah, it's *you*," he said when he saw Felix and me. "At breakfast I ask the kids if they like hot dogs for lunch, and they go crazy. So I fix the hot dogs just like you say."

He rang the lunch bell and there was an immedi-
ate stampede of kids behind us. We followed Mr. Kocsis into the dining hall. He took his place behind the
serving counter. I looked down at the trays of food.
All I saw was row after row of reddish, yellowish
mounds on top of hot dog buns.

"What *is* that?" Felix asked, a horrified look on
his face.

"My new American specialty," Mr. Kocsis
announced happily. "Hot dogs with sauerkraut and
paprika gravy!"

Lost Puppy

When I got home the next afternoon, I burst through the door and ran up to my bedroom with my bags. I had everything planned out: I'd ride my bike over to Shaw's Photo and Frame Shop, drop off the film I'd taken at camp, and pick up the photos of me and Mrs. Lawton. I'd pick one of the photos and put it in the frame I'd made for her. Then I'd ride over to her house and give her the gift.

No one was home at my house, but there was a note taped to my bedroom door. It said,

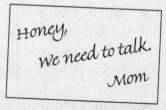

Honey,
 We need to talk.
 Mom

I pulled off the note, folded it, and stuck it in the back pocket of my jeans. Mom wasn't home now. I'd talk to her when I got a chance, but right now all I could think about was giving Mrs. Lawton her picture frame. I grabbed the brass 2 from where I'd left it on my bedside table and slipped it into my pocket.

I paid Mr. Shaw for the photos, and as soon as I got outside his shop, I ripped open the envelope and sorted through the photos inside. I was in a hurry, but I stopped dead in my tracks. The photos were amazing. They weren't like any picture of myself I'd ever seen. They were clearer and warmer, and they made me look good—which is no small feat. These photographs could have been in a magazine or on an album cover. I looked like a celebrity. It seemed like I was sitting in awkward positions when Mrs. Lawton was taking the photos, but in them I looked relaxed and natural. They were truly impressive.

Near the back of the deck, I found the photos of the two of us. It was tough, but I picked the one I liked best. In it, I was looking at Mrs. Lawton and laughing at something she'd said. She was laughing too, and her eyes were glimmering with mirth. I slipped the rest of the photos back in the envelope and put that one in the picture frame. It looked perfect. I couldn't wait for Mrs. Lawton to see it. I jumped back on my bike and pedaled as fast I could.

I ditched my bike in my driveway and headed up the street to Mrs. Lawton's house on foot. From down

the street I saw the silver Mercedes in Mrs. Lawton's
driveway. I was kind of disappointed that her son
would be there when I gave her my present, but it was
a good thing he was finally visiting her. They needed
to spend some time together.

I walked up the driveway, past the gleaming car. I
took one last look at the photo, and then climbed the
porch steps, holding the frame behind my back. The
front door was ajar. I rang the doorbell. In my excitement it seemed to take forever before I heard foot-
steps inside coming to the door. I was grinning like a
kid on Christmas morning.

The door was pulled open and a tall man looked
down at me. He was thin and had gray hair. He looked
tired. "Can I help you?" he asked.

"Is Mrs. Lawton here?" I asked him.

"Who are you?" he wanted to know.

"My name's Willie Plummet," I said. "Could you
tell Mrs. Lawton I'm here? She knows who I am."

"Oh, so *you're* Willie Plummet," the man said.

I smiled. I guess Mrs. Lawton had told him about
me. "Yes," I said. "May I come in? I just got back from
camp, and I have something to give her."

Mrs. Lawton's son looked down at me gravely a
moment. "I'm afraid that won't be possible," he said.
He looked at me sadly, like he wanted to tell me something without having to actually say it. It took a
moment, but then it hit me.

I took a step backwards. "Oh no," I said. "No, no, no."

The man nodded. "On Wednesday," he said. "She died peacefully in her sleep."

At those words, I felt my knees go weak.

"Wait here a moment," Mrs. Lawton's son told me. "There was something she left for you." He disappeared down the dark hallway.

I leaned against the door frame. I didn't know what I was feeling. I just began to shake all over. I couldn't seem to breathe right. Mrs. Lawton was gone.

In a moment, Mrs. Lawton's son was back. He handed me a large manila envelope. On the outside, in shaky handwriting, it said, "For the famous Willie Plummet." The flap had been torn open.

"I took a look inside," the man said. "It isn't anything valuable."

When the door closed, I turned and walked across the porch. Half way down the porch steps, I just sat down suddenly. My mouth was dry and I had a big lump in my throat. I looked down at the frame in my hands. *A friend loves at all times*. I'd thought I'd made the frame for her, but now I knew it was really for me.

I started to cry. Cars were driving by on the road, but I didn't care who saw. I just sat there sobbing, my nose running, my chest hurting. I'd only known Mrs. Lawton a short time, but I felt like I'd lost a lifelong friend. Sam's words came back to me: "Sometimes a few days is enough to really love something."

After a few moments, I stood up. I knew where I was going, but I don't remember walking there. I guess I was just wandering like some kind of lost pup. When I got to the park, the sun was going down. All the old people had gone home. I passed the run-down gazebo and the dead flower beds. A cool breeze swept across the sycamore trees. I walked down to the water's edge. The pond glimmered red and golden in the last light of day. I sat down on the steep bank, where Mrs. Lawton had stood to throw her stone. A few ducks floated serenely on the golden water.

I remembered the way Mrs. Lawton's stone bounced once on the surface when she threw it. I remembered how happy she looked at that moment. And for a moment, I smiled through the tears that still ran down my face. "You throw like a girl," I said aloud, as if she could hear me.

I stood up and pulled the brass 2 from my pocket. It was flat and heavy. I weighed it in my hand and looked out at the glimmering pond. "Let me show you how it's done," I said. I drew my arm back and sent the brass number spinning through the air. It sailed above the water in a beautiful curve, and then skipped magically a dozen or more times before it disappeared beneath the surface.

The cool breeze moved through my hair. I stood there smiling with my hands in my pockets and watched the splashes I'd made on the surface of the water disappear.

Then I turned and walked home.

Dog Tired

For the next few days, I stayed at home. The hot spell was back again, but I wasn't hanging around the house for the air conditioning; I just felt tired. I didn't watch TV or read. I didn't have the energy to do much of anything. I spent most of my time in my room.

On Wednesday, I finally went out to the garage and got a hammer and a few small nails. I took them up to my room and hammered a nail in my bedroom wall over my desk.

I took the picture of me and Mrs. Lawton out of my desk drawer. Under it, I found the manila envelope her son had given me. I'd completely forgotten about it. I set the envelope on my bed and hung the picture over my desk.

I stepped back to see if the picture was level. *A friend loves at all times.*

It was a wonderful photo. Mrs. Lawton's face was bright and cheerful. Her eyes were gleaming with laughter. I thought of that day on her front porch. I thought of all the time I'd spent in her parlor, telling her stories and making her laugh. I thought about our trip to the park. I was sad now, but I wouldn't trade those times for anything in the world. I was just thankful God had given me the opportunity to get to know her. And I knew I'd been a good friend to her. I hoped her last days on earth had been better because of me. I knew I would see her again, because we both shared a faith in Jesus Christ, and He had promised eternal life for both of us because of that faith.

I sat down on the bed, and noticed the manila envelope next to me. I picked it up and looked at it. "For the famous Willie Plummet," it read. I bent up the clasps and opened the flap to look inside. It was a very old letter in an envelope. I carefully pulled it out and looked at the envelope. It was addressed to Eudora Lawton in New York City. It smelled musty and dry.

I pulled out the letter and carefully unfolded it. It seemed about to fall apart along the creases. It was written in spidery handwriting with a fountain pen. It was a thank-you note from a man named Spiro Agnew for some photographs Mrs. Lawton had taken of him. I'd never heard of him, but I knew he must have been famous for Mrs. Lawton to leave me the letter.

I went downstairs, got the *A to Amsterdam* volume of the encyclopedia, and looked him up. He was vice president under Richard Nixon. There was only about a paragraph written about him. It was odd.

Why, of all the stuff Mrs. Lawton had, did she pick this letter to give me? I read the paragraph in the encyclopedia again to see if there was a clue there, but the choice still made no sense.

Maybe Mrs. Lawton gave it to me because she knew her son wouldn't want it. Hadn't he said he'd looked in the envelope to see what it was? If it was something valuable, he'd probably never have given it to me. Maybe Mrs. Lawton knew that, and she just wanted to give me something to remember her by.

I closed the encyclopedia and slipped it back into the bookshelf. It didn't really matter who had written the letter or how valuable it was; it was a gift from Mrs. Lawton, and that made it very valuable to me. I went back upstairs and looked at the photo hanging over my desk. There was still room enough up there for another frame.

The next day around noon I took the manila envelope down to Main Street on my bike. I parked my bike in front of Shaw's Photo and Framing and went inside. The bell above the door jingled as I pushed open the door. Mr. Shaw was on his lunch break, but his assistant, an old man with thick glasses, was behind the counter.

I set the manila envelope on the counter. "I'd like to have this framed," I told him. "It's a letter. Could you ask Mr. Shaw how much it will cost?"

The man looked at me over his glasses. "How would you like us to do it?" he asked. "We have a lot of different styles." He pointed up on the wall at the rows of framed photos and memorabilia.

I stepped closer to the wall and looked at the frames one by one. Some contained signed photos of celebrities. There were a few letters signed by presidents. Some frames contained rare stamps mounted and neatly matted.

I pointed at a simple metal frame with white matting. It looked like it was probably the least expensive. "How about this one?" I asked.

"Sure thing," the man said. "I'll have him call you."

The phone call from Mr. Shaw came that afternoon. Mom called me down to the kitchen phone.

"My assistant showed me your collectible," Mr. Shaw said. "I'd be happy to frame it free of charge. It would be an honor."

I felt so tired, it was hard to focus on what he was saying. "Well, thanks," I said, trying my best to sound appreciative. "That's very generous. When can I pick it up?"

"Not for a few days," he said. "I need to order some special non-acidic boards to mount it on and some special matting. You can come get it next Friday. And don't worry—it will be in the safe."

"Thank you, Mr. Shaw," I said into the phone. "Thank you very much."

The next few days I tried to get out of the house and keep myself busy, but I was still feeling tired. I went over to Sam's house, and went to the mall with Felix, but I wasn't very lively company. Sam and Felix were understanding, though.

On Friday I nearly forgot to go by the frame shop to pick up the letter Mrs. Lawton had given me. I got there just as Mr. Shaw was turning the sign in the window from open to closed. When he saw me, he hurriedly unlocked the door and pulled me inside.

"I was worried you wouldn't come," he told me excitedly, locking the door behind us again. "Wait right here. It's in the back."

Mr. Shaw disappeared into the back of the shop and came back in a few seconds carrying a large frame. "I've been a collector for years," he said, "and I've never seen anything like this—not here in Glenfield, anyway." What he said made no sense to me. He had a bunch of things up on his wall right now that were more impressive than the letter I'd given him to frame. He carried the frame toward me with the back turned, as if he wanted it to be a surprise.

It was.

He turned the frame around. He grinned. I looked at the fancy matting and the glittering gold frame that was far more impressive than the one I'd asked for. Inside the frame was the *envelope*, not the letter. I looked up at Mr. Shaw's face.

"Is something the matter?" he asked. "Have I done something wrong?"

I ran my fingers through my hair. "I really appreciate all your work," I told him, "but I wanted you to frame the letter, not the envelope."

Mr. Shaw's mouth dropped open. "You mean you don't know what you have here?"

I looked at the envelope in the frame. The answer seemed obvious. "It's an envelope," I said. "Isn't it?"

Mr. Shaw looked amazed. He shook his head and then looked at me again, closely, as if he was wondering if I was pulling his leg. "The *stamp*," Mr. Shaw said. "This is one of the *rarest* stamps in American collecting."

I stepped closer to the frame and looked at the stamp. It showed an American flag blowing in the wind. "Really?" I said. "*This* stamp?"

"They made a mistake on it," he said. "There aren't enough stars on the flag. Only a handful of these found their way into circulation." He smiled at me, disbelieving. "Do you have any idea how much this is worth?"

I peered at the stamp and shook my head.

"Why, I'd guess this stamp is worth 10,000 dollars," Mr. Shaw said. "Maybe more."

I looked at Mr. Shaw. He was grinning down at me. It hadn't sunk in.

"Willie Plummet," Mr. Shaw said. "You're the richest kid in town."

It turns out that the stamp was worth a lot more than even Mr. Shaw thought. He helped arrange an auction on the Internet, and I paid him some of the money we made. It took a while for the whole thing to seem real. Mrs. Lawton had left me her most valuable collectible, and she'd managed to do it without her son even realizing it. But who would have known how valuable that stamp was unless they took a close look at it? In a way, it was a lot like Mrs. Lawton herself.

By the time the check finally arrived in the mail, I'd already decided what to do with the money.

"You're crazy," Felix told me when I let him know my plans for the money. "If *I* had that kind of money I'd invest it in something guaranteed to make me a millionaire."

"Like tofu dogs?" I asked him.

Felix just laughed. He knew there was no way he'd change my mind.

The last Sunday of summer before school started again, I took my camera down to the park on Pickett Avenue. I stood and looked at the freshly painted gazebo and the flower beds with the magnolias in bloom. I looked at the new playground under the sycamores, with its swing set and slide. The grass in the park was green now, and the benches were all repaired. I walked past the new sign that said Lawton Park and went down to the duck pond.

It was a beautiful afternoon, and lots of people were enjoying the last days of summer. I sat at the edge of the pond for a while. I watched ducks float across the glimmering surface and listened to the voices of children up on the playground. I was waiting for the sun to start going down. When the shadows of the trees grew long, and the pond turned all golden and red, I stood up and took the lens cap off my camera.

I walked up through the park—the park that had been fixed up with the money I'd made from Mrs. Lawton's gift to me. It had never looked so good. The sun seemed to fill each leaf on the sycamore trees and seemed to glow within each blade of grass. It was time to take pictures.

I took a whole roll of film that day in the wonderful afternoon light Mrs. Lawton taught me to love. I took photos of an old man pushing a girl on the swings. I took photos of Mildred and Eunice, sitting on a bench chatting with two young sisters. I took a photo of a boy and an old man playing checkers.

I wasn't a great photographer like Mrs. Lawton, but I knew she would have liked them. ☼

Look for all these
exciting
WiLLiE PLummeT
misadventures
at your local
Christian
bookstore!